# Romeo
## for Real

# Romeo for Real

**MARKUS HARWOOD-JONES**

JAMES LORIMER & COMPANY LTD., PUBLISHERS
TORONTO

Copyright © 2018 by Markus Harwood-Jones
Published in the United States in 2018.

All rights reserved. No part of this book may be reproduced or transmitted in
any form or by any means, electronic or mechanical, including photocopying,
or by any information storage or retrieval system, without permission in writing
from the publisher.

James Lorimer & Company Ltd., Publishers acknowledges funding support
from the Ontario Arts Council (OAC), an agency of the Government of
Ontario. We acknowledge the support of the Canada Council for the Arts,
which last year invested $153 million to bring the arts to Canadians throughout
the country. This project has been made possible in part by the Government of
Canada and with the support of the Ontario Media Development Corporation.

Cover design: Shabnam Safari
Cover image: Shutterstock

978-1-4594-1298-9
eBook also available 978-1-4594-1297-2

Cataloguing data available from Library and Archives Canada.


Published by:
James Lorimer &
Company Ltd., Publishers
117 Peter Street, Suite 304
Toronto, ON, Canada
M5V 0M3
www.lorimer.ca

Distributed in the US by:
Lerner Publisher Services
1251 Washington Ave. N.
Minneapolis, MN, USA
55401
www.lernerbooks.com


Printed and bound in Canada.
Manufactured by Friesens Corporation in Altona, Manitoba,
Canada in December 2017.
Job # 239689

*For you.*

# 01 Sweet Victory

SMOKE TRICKLED OUT of the car into the night air. It followed the sounds of three young men's voices as they cruised the street. It was Friday night, and they were winners.

"Coach almost blew it," said Ben as he tossed a cigarette butt out the driver-side window. "Should have had me guarding 22 for the whole game."

"Did you see the look on his face at the

buzzer?" Marty grinned from ear to ear. "I swear, he was gonna cry!"

Ben took a quick glance over his shoulder and changed lanes. "That guy's gotta learn to have a little faith. Oh, and Rome, that was a nice three-pointer you stuck in at the end."

"Thanks." Rome leaned back. "For a sec I thought I'd short-armed it. The guy's hand was right in my face. Thanks for the pass."

The car slowed as Ben eased into the fast-food drive-through. "It's what I do." He laughed. "That and give nightmares to sissies like 22!"

Still leaning into the back seat, Rome watched his friends and sighed. Ben was lazily resting one hand on the wheel. Marty pulled on a joint in the front seat, laughing loudly. His braces made his grin glint silver. *Remember this moment*, Rome told himself. *This is the one you want to hold on to.*

This was it. Every drop of sweat and extra hour of practice had been worth it. Now there was no doubt their team would go down in high-school history.

They had the matching team jackets, a new banner for the gym, and class rings glittering on their fingers. Rome tried to smile. He couldn't figure out why his eyes were welling up instead. *Must be the smoke*, he figured. He wiped his face with his sleeve before his friends could see.

A shaky voice from the drive-through speaker asked for their order.

"What do you want?" Ben asked, leaning back to catch Rome's answer. Rome just shrugged.

"Fine, you'll have what I'm having," Ben decided. He turned to the speaker. "Two double cheeseburger combos, extra ketchup."

"And a fish burger!" added Marty with a shout.

"Fish burgers are gay," Ben teased as he pulled around to pay.

"Screw you," Marty barked back. "They're not gay, they're kosher, dickhead."

At the window, a bored-looking brunette waited with their food and drinks. Ben gave her a wink and said, "And how much to take you home?"

Her face remained blank as she passed over their meals.

As they sped away, Ben flashed a smile. "She was totally into me."

"Yeah, right," laughed Marty. Rome noticed he already had bits of fish burger caught in his braces. "Pretty sure it was me she was scoping."

Rome reached forward and plucked the joint from Marty's fingers. He silently judged his friends. *I swear, any time we're around a cute girl these two just lose their heads. Grow up already, guys.*

The window was open a crack, and Rome could feel a touch of cool air. As they passed over the bridge he watched the Winnipeg skyline and the dark waters of the Red River swirling below. His head began to feel fluffy, his thoughts looser. A smile crept to his lips.

"Thanks for the food, Ben," Rome said, unwrapping his burger.

"Anytime," Ben replied.

Rome bit into his burger and let his mind slip away. He soaked in the mindless chatter of the evening.

Marty and Ben told and retold details of their own athletic feats. They relived every moment of the last game, then went over the whole season.

"You remember that bank shot I made back in first year?" Ben bragged.

Marty rolled his eyes. "You were a total bricklayer back then."

"First day of PE," Ben continued, as if Marty hadn't said a word. "That's when Coach told me I was his first choice for power forward."

"That's bull!" Marty groaned. "You were benched most of first year, just like the rest of us!"

"I threw off my ankle, right before the first game," Ben replied lightly. "But Coach said he wanted me at his side, even if I couldn't play."

"As if!" Marty laughed.

The two bickered, their stories becoming as repetitive as the scenery. Squat apartment blocks, dollar stores, fast-food joints, and laundromats ran up and down the streets off St. Mary's Road. Rome looked up at the empty, overcast night sky, then down at his class ring, which shimmered in the city's bright lights. *This is it*, he thought. *This is the last time it'll ever be like this.*

Marty's voice broke into Rome's thoughts. Prodding his knee, "What you daydreaming about back there?" Marty asked, prodding his knee.

"What is he ever thinking about? I bet it's Rosie again, isn't it?" Ben teased. He caught Rome's eye in the rear-view mirror. "Bet you're gonna get it tonight, eh, buddy?"

Rome felt himself start to grow red. Damn, why did he have to blush so easily? He ran a hand through his thick hair.

"Where was she tonight, anyway?" asked Marty.

Rome coughed and tried to find his words. "She, uh, actually —" But before he could say any more, Rome was interrupted. Ben waved to get his friends' attention and pointed to some people on the sidewalk.

"Check it out," Ben said in a loud whisper. "Couple of body-builder butt-munchers!"

Rome followed his friend's gaze and spied two massive guys, both bald. They wore tight-fitting black tank tops and walked side by side. They would have been relatively uninteresting if it wasn't for one fact — they were holding hands! Marty started to giggle at the sight. But Ben didn't look so pleased. When the car pulled up to a red light, the couple were barely a stone's throw away, and getting closer.

Ben got a wicked look. He motioned for Rome to pass up his fast-food trash. "Watch this," Ben grinned. He crumpled up their used napkins, wrappers, and empty bags. He told Marty to take the lid off his pop and dipped it all in.

Rome played along, welcoming the distraction. He leaned out the back window to whistle. "Hey, boys!"

As the two large men turned their heads, Ben pelted them with the wads of sticky paper. Following suit, Marty grabbed his drink and threw it in the couple's direction. All three boys in the car laughed as the cup exploded over the men in a marvellous sticky mess. They sped away as the light turned green, squealing off into the night.

Rome's laughter was just as loud as Marty's and Ben's. But it left a foul taste in his mouth. His stomach began to clench, and his hands grew sweaty. *Catholic brainwashing, I guess*, he thought. *Always feeling guilty for having fun.*

Rome stuck his head into the cool breeze coming through the window. He let the lights of the city blur together. A sigh escaped him and was swallowed up by the rush of air. Feeling teary again, he closed his eyes. He wouldn't break down — not tonight. This was a night to celebrate, to make memories that would last a lifetime. He would not let himself ruin it.

# 02 *Sloppy Seconds*

ROME PUSHED THE FRIES around in his half-eaten poutine. *What's wrong with me?* he scolded himself as he munched on the chunky cheese curds. *Why couldn't I just love her?* The words were caught in his mind like a bad song stuck on repeat. He shook his head, glaring down at his food like it was somehow responsible.

A hand reached out and nabbed a fry. It snapped Rome out of his sulking stupor. "Mornin', bro."

15

"Is it still that early?" Rome moaned. He didn't bother to look up.

As Ben sat down across from Rome in the diner booth, he reached for another helping of his food.

"Dude, it's noon. Have you been here all day? These fries are cold!" Ben shovelled Rome's second-hand fries into his mouth. "What's up, man? Stuff going on with you and Rosie?"

"More like lack thereof . . ." Rome mumbled. He watched the grey clouds outside the dirty diner window as they slowly worked their way across the wide-open Winnipeg sky. *He'll never understand*, thought Rome. *Not now, not after all this time. But I have to tell him something.*

Ben raised his eyebrows.

Finally, after a long silence, Rome spoke. He kept his gaze fixed on the window. "Apparently, I'm not her 'type.'" He felt his face begin to blush and he stood up quickly. "Whatever. I was just leaving."

"Then I'll come," Ben said, standing. He pushed most of the remaining fries into his mouth and threw a ten on the table to cover the food.

Rome didn't answer. He was already taking quick strides toward the door. A bell rang as he left the little diner and made his way to his car. It rang again as Ben followed after him.

"Just tell me the deal, what happened?" Ben demanded. He sped up so he could walk by Rome's side. Ben leaned against Rome's car door. "Dammit! Look, I'm trying to be a friend, asshole."

Rome let out a frustrated sigh. "Dude, it's just . . ." He bit his lip. "It's Rosie. She's seeing . . . Someone else." Rome's cheeks burned again.

Raindrops began to fall around them, dotting the sidewalk and the shoulders of Rome's jacket. Ben didn't seem to even notice the weather. He scowled at Rome intensely. "What's the bastard's name?! We'll kick his ass!"

Rome looked down at his shoes in defeat. Puddles began to form on the concrete. "Lyla," he admitted. "She's with some chick named Lyla."

Ben's mouth was a thin line for half a second.

Then he broke into a roaring laugh. "She's a rug-muncher?!" Ben doubled over, overcome with laughter long enough for Rome to shove him off the car.

"I told you, leave me alone," Rome said in a huff.

Ben pulled himself together enough to respond between bouts of giggles. "Look, forget her, man. There are plenty of hot girls in the city, you'll find one." There was a pause before he added, "So long as they don't all just hook up with each other first!" Ben cracked up again, letting Rome make his getaway.

Rome's mind raced as fast as his car. *What is wrong with me?!* He felt himself tearing up, then a hot flash of anger ran across his face. *Rosie is the perfect girl. Everyone could see it. We were meant for each other! But I just couldn't do it, I couldn't even make a move!* Guilt began to pool in the pit of his stomach as he thought of Ben, Marty, his friends on the team. Even his parents. *I lied to all of them, letting them think I was normal. Why can't I just be normal?*

As he pulled into his driveway, Rome sank forward. He rested his head on the steering wheel as his mind raced with memories. Nights up late, snuggling with Rosie and watching old movies. Days at school, passing notes in class. Summer vacations, lazing on the top of his car, the two of them counting stars. They'd been friends for so long, everyone just knew they were meant to be together. But whenever Rome tried to imagine making a move, he found it wasn't Rosie he dreamed of.

His mind began to wander to those late-night thoughts, the ones that made his skin tingle with excitement. A figure pulling him closer. Hands running along his sides. A voice whispering in his ear . . .

Rome sat up in a cold sweat. He stepped out of the car and hurried inside. Brushing past his mother, he made his way downstairs to the bathroom. Those shameful thoughts were the issue. This was how he'd ended up in this whole mess. He would not get sucked into them again. "What the hell is wrong with you?" Rome scolded himself in the mirror. He splashed cold water on his face before taking the few steps to his room and throwing himself into bed.

Rome tried to take a nap, but instead he just spaced out, caught up in a storm of worried thoughts. After a long while, he gave up and rolled over, glancing at his phone. He had a voicemail. From Rosie.

"Look, I'm sorry I haven't called in a little while. I'd really like us to stay friends. I miss — uh, I mean . . . You know what I mean. Anyway, um, look. Did you want to come to my new place tonight? I'm doing a thing. There'll be people, drinks, that kind of stuff. She's gonna be there. I want you to meet her. Lyla, I mean. I hope you come. Just . . . don't bring anyone, please. Just you. See you later, I guess. I'm texting you the address. Um, oh, and it starts at eight. Come by whenever, I guess . . . Okay, bye."

Rome listened to the message again. And then again. He pulled a repurposed pop bottle from under his bed and took a swig. The harsh sting of alcohol hit the back of his throat. Staring at the minutes passing on his phone, Rome thought it over. "Well, drinking at a party is better than staying in and drinking alone," he said to himself.

*Or worse*, he thought, *Getting drunk by myself while my folks upstairs do the same.* It was getting late on Saturday night. It was prime time for alcohol-induced emotional avoidance in the Montague household.

Checking his Friend Findr app, he saw that Ben was at Marty's place. No surprise there. The phone rang twice before Marty answered. Rome could hear Ben giggling in the background. They were probably already laughing about Rosie and her new partner. "You with Ben?" Rome asked, knowing the answer.

"We're going to a party. At Rosie's."

"Dyke Rosie?!" Ben called out from the background.

Rome rolled his eyes. Maybe Rosie was right — he probably should just go alone. But it was too late now. Talking over the giggling on the other side of the line, Rome asked, "You coming or not?"

He could hear Ben take the phone from Marty. "Two conditions," Ben said.

"Sure, whatever," Rome replied. It was just like Ben to have 'conditions' for a good time.

"One. We're all gonna hit up this lesbo party and score some hot bi chicks." Rome could hear Marty cracking up. Ben continued over the laughter. "Two. Rome, my man, we are gonna make sure you get some action — from someone who isn't Rosie!"

"Whatever, dude," Rome answered. He was barely listening.

"I'm serious," said Ben. "You need some closure, bro."

"Fine," Rome agreed, standing to leave, "I'll pick you up."

Ben's car made its way down St. Mary's Road. By the time it had crossed over the bridge, the trio's nervous giggles had turned into nervous silence. As they moved deeper into the city, they began to pass people sitting on piles of blankets, asking for change. Pubs blared angry-sounding music. Rough-looking bikers crowded around broken-down motels, smoking cigarettes. Up ahead was the stocky apartment building with the address Rosie had texted to Rome.

They were up the stairs in moments. There was a fresh rainbow sticker next to the number on the door. Rome and his buddies shared a nervous chuckle before knocking on the worn-down wood. Inside, someone yelled, "I'll get it!"

A girl opened the door, or maybe it was a boy? Rome wasn't sure. The stranger had a woman's voice, but also had a small black soul patch on his — her? — chin. The stranger looked them up and down, frowning. Rome hesitated, but it was too late to back out.

"We're friends of Rosie," Ben announced, pushing past the person at the door. Marty shrugged and stepped in behind Ben. Rome looked down and followed his friends inside.

# 03 *Fireworks*

"ARE WE THE ONLY GUYS HERE?" Marty asked, leaning in to loudly whisper at the other two.

"The only real guys," Ben scoffed. "This is like a rave for gay strippers."

Marty snorted. Rome saw Ben's point. Nearly everyone had colourful streaks in their hair and were rocking shaved sides, glimmering piercings, and a variety of tattoos. Even the bigger ones wore tight, revealing clothes with denim or leather jackets. A few even had on fishnets. Most did look like girls. Probably girls, at least. There were a few girly looking guys too. And there were plenty, like the one at the door, that Rome couldn't really figure out.

Rome awkwardly pushed his way across the room. He headed for the table with snacks and booze, and dropped down the six pack Ben had scored. He popped open a can, trying to blend in.

At first, Rome stuck close to his boys. The three of them, marked by their matching athletic jackets, moved as a unit. But after a few laps around the room and a few drinks, he began to relax. An hour in, the trio had moved apart. Rome watched Ben talking up a tall goth girl on the couch. She was practically sitting on his lap. Ben's act, which usually drove girls away, seemed to make her smile. Rome spied Marty leaning on the wall, checking his braces in the reflection of his class ring.

Rome was hanging near the drinks table when he spotted Rosie. She stood on the balcony, lit cigarette in hand. She had been so busy with her other guests she hadn't even noticed him come in. She'd been out there since they arrived, smoking like a chimney. She would finish one, flick the butt over the railing, and light another. Sometimes she paused to whisper into the ear of the girl on her arm. Rome felt a burning in his belly. He bit his lip as the hot feeling worked its way up to his face. "That's fine," Rome mumbled into his drink. "I didn't really wanna talk anyway."

Rome turned his attention back to Marty. Now he was chatting with someone — the short, squat girl who had let them into the party. Or was that a guy? Rome couldn't be bothered to try to figure it out anymore.

Rome let his gaze wander to Ben. Ben was all but straddling the goth girl on the couch. Rome turned back to Marty, who was looking sweaty and awkward as all hell as that girl-guy got closer and closer to him.

Around this time, Rome noticed the room was starting to sway. His drink was empty, so he reached for another. He poured himself a shot of someone else's liquor. The familiar burn felt good going down his throat.

Rome began to work through the crowd, making his way toward the balcony. He was dying to talk to Rosie, just to be near her again. He wanted her to know he'd come. He wanted to tell her he wanted to stay friends. *Just friends*, he admitted to himself. *Even if everyone else thought we were boyfriend and girlfriend, we knew we were just friends. And that's enough. I just want my friend back.*

Rosie looked happy. Her red hair flew when she tossed her head back in a laugh as the woman on her arm whispered in her ear. Part of Rome was happy, too. It was good to see her smile like that. But his happiness for her was followed by a pang of jealousy. She had found it. She had found someone who could love her like she deserved to be loved. Rome wondered if that would ever happen for him.

Rome tried to hurry to get to Rosie. He pushed people aside. He kept having to swerve or side-step through the crowd. By the time he had a clear view of the balcony, Rosie was gone.

Just then, someone behind him shouted, "You're

a what?! What?!" Rome whirled around to see Ben pushing the goth girl to the floor. She scrunched down and looked like she was about to cry. "She said she — she's a man!" Ben howled.

Rome shook his head. Rosie was right. He never should have brought these guys. They were sure to cause trouble.

Rome just stayed on the balcony, hoping Rosie might come back. He bummed a smoke and lit it without so much as a 'thanks.' He closed his eyes as he inhaled, tuning out. Somewhere, far away, there was the sound of shouting and the slamming of a door. It didn't matter as long as he was sucking in that familiar toxic taste. Soon enough, the ember was down to his fingers. He opened his eyes in surprise as it burned him. He let the remains of the filter fall. He watched it tumble down to the street until it hit the pavement, the orange sparks flying out like tiny fireworks.

Rome ducked back inside and turned down the apartment's only hallway, hoping to catch a glimpse of Rosie. Sadly, all he found was the line to the bathroom. There was no sign of her. No help from his friends. He was stranded in a room full of strangers he couldn't understand. Turning, he opened the only other door in the hall. *This whole night has just been a waste*, thought Rome. He closed his eyes and exhaled in relief as the door shut behind him. At last, he could just be alone again.

After a moment, he looked up. He figured he was in Rosie and her girlfriend's bedroom. There were piles of clothes on the floor and a few unpacked boxes. Books and films with titles like *Unspeakable Things* and *A Full Guide to Lesbian Sex* were scattered around. But the most curious part of the room was the other person in it. A young man, head in his hands, sat at the edge of the bed.

As soon as he saw him, the pounding in Rome's head stopped. Along with everything else. The stranger's shy eyes peering out from under his bangs. He stared up at Rome like a deer in headlights. Rome couldn't look away.

As the stranger pulled his hands from his face, Rome noticed his knuckles were splashed with colourful paint. The splatters matched the rainbow of spots that ran across his flannel shirt and dark skinny jeans. A spark ran through Rome's body as he thought about what it might be like to have those hands on him. *Where did that come from?* he briefly wondered.

The stranger finally spoke. "Hi."

Rome's mind went blank. He was a boat floating freely in a vast ocean. The buzz of his drunken state buoyed him toward uncharted seas. The stranger's dark eyes pulled him in like whirlpools. Rome's body grew warmer, like it was waking up, brimming with excitement. The stranger came forward, reaching up to touch Rome's cheek. A burst of desire rang through Rome's chest, washing away any doubt he still might have had.

"I'm Romeo," he said, without thinking. Then he felt silly. "Um, I mean, nobody really calls me that. Except my mom, I guess." The name felt strange in his mouth, awkward, too big for him to swallow back. He didn't understand why he had said it that way. He didn't understand much of anything at this point. "Rome — it's just Rome," he corrected. He stammered over his words as he tried to explain. "I mean, it's actually Romeo Montague. Pretty much everyone just calls me Rome. But you could call me Romeo, I guess, if you wanted to . . ."

"Romeo," said the stranger. He held the name in his mouth as if to savour the taste. Rome felt his whole body shiver. The young man pushed his fingers into Rome's hair. Rome could feel the warmth of his breath. With little more than a heartbeat between the two of them, Rome leaned in.

Rome had read that a kiss was supposed to feel like fireworks, like church bells, like waterfalls. He'd seen it in movies. He'd spent a long time trying to guess how it might be with Rosie. But this wasn't like anything he could have planned. It was like a drink of water when he'd been thirsty for years. All he could think was that he needed more. The world was spinning and they were at the centre of everything. Rome and this stranger. Rome held him close, never wanting this moment to end.

# 04 Rough Awakening

A SUDDEN PUSH FROM BEHIND forced Rome to the floor. The two boys fell. Rome landed awkwardly on top.

A voice from above growled, "There's the bastard." The owner of the voice tapped Rome's shoulder. "You think it's funny to pick on fags?"

Rome scrambled to his feet. In front of him stood a familiar bald, buff man. Rome's stomach turned into knots and he found himself wordless. It was the same guy Rome and his buddies had pelted on the sidewalk.

"Get. Out," the man snarled.

He didn't need to say it twice. Rome turned for one last look at the young man on the floor, offering a sorry glance. Then he took off running.

*Shit, shit, shit!* Rome could barely think anything else as he raced down the stairs. Adrenaline was sloshing in his stomach, mixing sourly with the booze. The guys were waiting for him, smoking by the car.

Rome crawled in to the passenger's seat without a word. The trio made their way home, back to their safe, normal, straight neighbourhood.

At last, alone in his room, Rome lay awake. He rolled back and forth but couldn't get comfortable. Every time he tried to close his eyes, there was the stranger, his warm body pushing up against him, his teeth tenderly pulling at Rome's lower lip, his firm hips grinding . . . Rome opened his eyes. His body was tingling in frustration.

Pushing himself up in bed, Rome shook his head. He smacked a hand against his face, trying to wake up. "I was drunk," he told himself. "Drunk and lonely. That's it." But as he lay back down, he knew the truth. More than anything, he wanted to do it all over again.

A tiny smile found its way to his face as he was pulled back into the fantasy. In the moment, it had felt so vivid. But now it was like trying to relive a dream. *No*, Rome corrected himself, *a nightmare*.

He decided he might as well give up on drifting off peacefully. Rome leaned over and reached under his bed for his pop bottle full of whiskey. It made him cough and destroyed whatever was left of his toothpaste's minty freshness. Rome caught his breath and went back for another swig.

Rome stood up in front of his full-length mirror and looked at himself. He flexed his arms, pulled at his eyes, traced his fingers along his rough jawline. He didn't look gay. He looked like he always had, the same as yesterday. His black hair, tossed into a mess. His brown eyes, tinted with the redness of being tired and drunk. He stared down the reflection, daring it to change. But it just stood there, staring back. All the same.

Rome wavered, grasping the bottle with both hands. He was consumed by a fire inside him that the booze couldn't douse. Through his stupor, he felt the room start to spin. When he closed his eyes, his fantasies were waiting for him. They had haunted Rome for far too long. They found their way into the moments when he was too tired or drunk to care. These thoughts were the ones that had kept him from falling for Rosie. Or any other girl, for that matter.

A figure reached out, wrapping Rome in his arms. Rome couldn't fight it anymore. Rome saw, for the first time, it wasn't a woman. Or even a man. It was a person, one who looked exactly like that beautiful, curious stranger from Rosie's party. Finally, Rome let go.

Slowly, Rome's eyes fluttered open. It was brighter than he'd expected. Sprawled on the floor, he felt like he'd been to hell and back. Last night had felt so unreal, he couldn't help but wonder if it was all a dream. He staggered up, face to face with his reflection again. It wasn't as scary in the light of day. He tossed his secret booze bottle back under his bed to nestle among pages of forgotten homework.

A wave of nausea hit. Rome dragged himself to the bathroom, listening for his parents' footsteps upstairs. He kneeled over the toilet. The booze burned just as hard as it came back up. At least a few shots made their way out of him before he flushed the toilet. He brushed the residue off his teeth and washed off the face of the night before. Then he wandered back into his room and plopped onto his bed again.

"I kissed a boy," he said out loud. "And I liked it." It was like finding a puzzle piece and then stepping back, finally able to see the whole picture.

So much made sense now. At the same time, Rome realized, there was so much he didn't know. He decided he had to talk to someone about what had happened to him, what he finally knew. He reached for his phone and ran through the list of his most frequent contacts.

Ben? Not a chance. He could hear Ben calling him Faggot Romie just like he had nicknamed Dyke Rosie. Hell, Ben might even try to beat the gay out of him. The guy wasn't a saint. Rome had seen Ben get into fights once or twice. But he'd never had to face him head on and wasn't eager to do so. Even in a best-case scenario, Ben would probably think Rome was coming on to him.

Marty? Maybe. He was nice, open-minded-ish. But not enough. Marty would be perfect for some things. To confess to about girl trouble, weird personal stuff, or if his dad flew off the handle. But this was something else altogether. And Marty made gay jokes too, going along with whatever Ben did. Of course, Rome did too . . .

Finally, it struck him. Rome knew exactly who he should call! She'd been through this same situation, more or less. Too excited to wait, he dialed her immediately. The ringer went twice before a groggy voice answered, "Hello?" She sounded like Rome had woken her up. But he shrugged. This was too important.

"Hey, Rosie." He paused for a second before adding, "Don't hang up."

"What do you want?" Rosie asked harshly. "Are you drunk? Do you even know what time it is?" He heard another voice complaining that it was too early to answer the phone.

"No! I mean, maybe. But I . . ." Rome didn't know exactly how to say it. Or what he was planning to say at all. "I need to talk to you. It's important. It's not anything to do with us, I promise. Really, really important, actually. Can we meet up?" His hands were wet and shaking from a mix of nerves and hangover.

"I guess . . . Lyla?" Rosie said, her voice a little distant. "Brunch?"

There was a muffled conversation on the other end. Rome waited, shuffling his feet. Finally, Rosie came back to the phone. "Meet us at the café near our place. I'll text you the deets. But I'm going back to sleep first."

"Sure, perfect. See you soon," Rome replied in haste. He hung up without even a goodbye. Why did Lyla have to be there? Rome frowned. He barely knew her. He definitely couldn't talk about all this in front of a stranger!

Sighing, Rome crawled back into the bedsheets. Rosie was right, it was too early for this. Too tired to keep fighting, Rome allowed himself to dream. He felt himself slipping into close embraces, quivering lips, and the desire he'd found in the arms of that nameless man.

# 05 A Warm Welcome

THE NAME OF THE PLACE was on the purple awning: Gayley's Café. Rome rolled his eyes. Still, Rosie was waiting for him, so he wasn't about to turn back now, not without at least a coffee and a nice, greasy breakfast. Swallowing his pride, Rome approached the restaurant.

He could see Lyla and Rosie through the window. First, a wave of happiness washed over Rome. *They look good together*, he thought. Then, a second wave hit. This one was harder to understand. Jealousy? Fear? Resentment? Why was it so easy for them, and so hard for him?

Rosie unlocked eyes with Lyla for a moment. She looked up and waved at Rome. Taking a deep breath, Rome walked up to the couple. There was just a moment of hesitation in his step.

"Uh, hi," said Rome. He offered a meek wave to Lyla, who nodded in return. Without a word, Rosie stood and hugged him. Rome wrapped himself around her and a whimper escaped him. "It's so good to see you," he choked.

Rosie let go and gave a gentle smile. "I've missed you, buddy."

Lyla watched them both carefully. She gave Rome a thin smile when he finally took a seat. "I've heard a lot about you," she said with another nod.

Rome assessed Lyla. It was the first time he'd seen her up close. Other than the hint of tired bags hanging under her eyes, she seemed perfectly put together. A touch of gold makeup highlighted her cheeks, making her dark skin sparkle in the morning light. Her soft curls floated just above her shoulders. As she reached for Rosie's hand, Rome noticed her wrists were covered with shimmering bands and bangles.

Rosie reached out and tapped Rome's hand sympathetically. Unlike Lyla, Rosie looked like she had been up all night. Her fierce red hair was piled into a messy bun and heavy bags rested under her eyes, standing out against her pale skin. She wore a wrinkled flannel shirt with the sleeves rolled up and, as she took Lyla's hand, Rome noticed she had on bracelets to match Lyla's. There was something else too, something about her. It was a sort of glow. Rome saw Rosie's cheeks turn pink as she caught her lover's eye. Rome looked away, feeling himself flush.

Even when looking down, Rome could feel it as the two women turned to look him over. He bit his cheek, chewing over what to say next. "So, Rosie," he began, not able to meet her eyes.

"Actually," Rosie said, "it's just Rose now."

"Oh." That would take some getting used to.

Silence sat between them for a while. Then Rosie spoke up again. "Look, you got us out here. Why did you need to talk, like, now-now-now?"

"No, it's not, um, well . . . It's just, I-I think . . ." Rome stumbled, searching for the words. He glanced up, his eyes darting back and forth between the two girls. "So, you're gay."

Rosie smirked at Lyla. "Well, we are . . ." she said, "very happy." Lyla winked back at Rosie.

"What's . . . what's it like? I mean, how did you figure it out?" This was a lot easier when they were talking about Rosie instead of Rome.

"Well . . ." Rosie began, smiling. "We met, we talked, we clicked. We started hanging out a lot. And after a lot of thinking, and talking, and a bit of kissing . . ." Her cheeks turned pink again. "I just sort of realized that I really liked Lyla." She shrugged. "I mean, you must have figured, right? I'm such a lesbian!"

Rosie beamed. Lyla looked at her with pride. Rome cringed. Now that that part of the discussion was over, it was time to talk about him. Closing his eyes, Rome blurted out, "I kissed someone at your party."

"You're not the one who messed with Paris last night, are you?" Lyla spoke up. "I heard some transphobic prick tried to put the moves on her." She gave Rome a stern look.

Rome laughed nervously. "No, I don't think that was me. Honestly, I don't even know his name." All Rome could feel was the hotness in his cheeks. He muttered, "I . . . I think I'm gay . . . or something. I don't know. Whatever."

Rosie's eyes grew wide. Rome could see shock in her face. But excitement too. She gasped, "No! Really?! That's awesome! Way to go, Romie!" Rosie squealed.

Rome just squirmed in his seat. "Thanks, Rosie," he mumbled.

"It sounds like you're learning a lot about yourself right now," Lyla chimed in, tapping her fingertips on the side of her coffee cup. "Rosie's right, that's awesome, and there's also no need to rush into a label."

Lyla motioned to herself, setting her bracelets jangling. "Like, I thought I was straight for a long time. So, when I realized I wasn't, I was pretty confused, and it took me a while to figure myself out. These days, I call myself pansexual."

Rome gave Lyla a sideways glance. Was that the word for some kind of fetish?

Lyla read his blank expression and began to laugh. "Pan? No? Oh geez, you really are a gaybie!" Rosie gave her a wry look. "Right, right." Lyla smirked. "Well, the point is — I get it! Just know there's options out there. You might be bi, pan, ace, or queer. Or something else altogether!"

Rome's shoulders slumped as he looked out the window. Ben's voice in his head was cracking mean jokes. He felt like Lyla was making fun of him, using made-up words. He was still hungover and it was all getting to be a bit too much.

Rosie reached across the table to tap his hand and bring him back. "She's right, Romie. Just let yourself like who you like. You can figure out the rest later."

Lyla fished through her purse, saying, "I had a feeling you might be on our team." She pulled out a bright yellow pamphlet with a rainbow across the top and held it out to him.

Rome eyed the paper cautiously.

Rosie rolled her eyes. "It's for the Rainbow City Centre. Plus there's a list of all the friendly places in town, plus a bunch of events and stuff!" She smiled widely, showing off the little gap between her teeth. "They've got something for everyone! Even your parents and friends!"

"Okay, no, Rosie — er, Rose. Just — hold up a second," Rome said, putting his hands up in defense. He looked around to make sure no one was listening in. "You think I'm gonna actually tell my parents and friends?!"

"There must've been a reason you couldn't wait to tell us," said Rose.

"Well, it was just . . ." Rome stumbled over his explanation. "I just needed someone to talk to."

"Look, I get it," Rose offered. "My parents didn't

exactly take it very well. They're still calling Lyla my 'roommate.'" She rolled her eyes at the very thought.

"Still," Lyla added, "if you plan to go around kissing mysterious men at parties . . . well, you might want to consider what to do when people find out, rather than if."

Rose took the pamphlet off the table and pushed it into Rome's hands. "Just take the damn thing, Romie! You might want to get to know your community. It's a pretty fabulous one!"

"Could you not say things like that?" Rome shot her a look as he shoved the paper deep into his pocket.

"Things like what?" Rose asked smugly.

"You know . . ." Rome looked away. "Like, 'fabulous' or whatever," he grumbled.

He didn't want to be that kind of gay guy. Of course, what other kind was there? He felt confused again, and his head started pounding. He drank the rest of his lukewarm coffee in a single gulp. But it didn't help. "I don't — I'm not like that. Even if I'm gay, or something."

"Oh, sweet baby-queer." Lyla shook her head.

"Not all gay men prance around in leotards and feather boas. Though, I've seen it done." She chuckled. "It's just like how not all lesbians wear plaid and ride motorbikes."

Rose smirked. "I was thinking of getting a motorized scooter."

Lyla and Rose shared a giggle. Rome just crossed his arms. Eventually, Lyla turned back to Rome and said, "It's all about pride in who you are, not acting out some script."

"I guess so." Rome shrugged.

Rose grinned. "And if you do want a boa or some glitter, I can hook you up!"

Rome smiled weakly. "Thanks. I mean, no thanks on the boa and all. But thanks." He pulled the pamphlet back out and uncrumpled it. He looked at the list of cafés, walk-in clinics, and small businesses. "So, now what?"

Rose just shrugged. Lyla said simply, "Welcome to the team."

# 06 Reconnection

THE ORCHARD BOOKSTORE had rainbows everywhere, mixed in with many other flags Rome didn't recognize. One was purple, green, and yellow. One faded from pink to blue. Several had symbols as strange to him as ancient runes. Rome read the pamphlet again, confirming the address. But there was no doubt this was the place. *Maybe I shouldn't have come*, he thought, biting his lip.

Rome wandered through the shelves. He browsed

each section like he was on an archaeological dig. He scanned the titles with guilty fascination. There were so many books. They were squeezed on the shelves in such a way that he worried pulling on one would make the ones beside it explode out with it. Many were simply piled on the floor or sitting on their sides on top of other shelves. Once or twice he had to catch himself from bumping into things and tipping over several of the small stacks.

Rome carefully avoided sections with names like Lesbian Erotics, Queer Spirituality, and Trans Lit. He moved toward the more familiar. In Classic Fiction (where the 'i's were dotted with little pink hearts), he found a copy of *Frankenstein*. When he opened it, he found it was a retelling of the original, made to be about politically radical transsexuals. He put the book down on top of a rather high stack and moved on to gaze over more titles.

Voices floated over from the other side of the shelf and Rome couldn't help but eavesdrop. Here were some real gays, in their natural element.

He felt like a wildlife researcher. Listening through the stacks, Rome caught hints of conversation, giggling, and teasing. *They almost sound like me, Marty, and Ben*, he thought. As the group grew quiet, Rome began to worry they would leave before he could catch a glimpse. Unable to find a peephole, he decided to make his own.

Rome picked up a novel and set it on top of a nearby stack. He removed another after that, and continued removing books one by one. He tried not to be noticed. The shopkeeper was busy talking to someone and barely glanced in his direction, but Rome kept an eye out, just in case. Finally, when he had cleared his side of the shelf, he ducked down for a look. But he found himself face to face with more books, this time with the spines pointed away from him. *Of course!* He slapped his own forehead at his short-sighted thinking.

Then Rome heard a voice. What was that? He could swear someone was saying his name! Urgently, he tried to pull one of the books from the other side of the shelf. He pinched at the paper with his forefingers, but he only managed to push the books over. They fell with a handful of soft thumps. Rome ducked down before he could even glance through the opening. There were light treads, footsteps approaching the other side of the shelf. Someone had noticed him. He peered up to see a familiar face.

"You!" Rome exclaimed at the same time as the familiar stranger. Rome felt his face turn red. He wondered if he'd been hit on the head and had slipped into a very vivid dream. The mystery boy was here, right in front of him! Rome looked down quickly, shoving his sweaty palms into his pockets. What were the chances? What should he even say? *What if he doesn't like me? What if he does like me?!*

The boy took a step closer and said, "Romeo, that's you, isn't it?"

Worried thoughts flitted through Rome's mind while he stumbled over a few words, "I, um — it's, um —"

The stranger placed his hand on the edge of the shelf and peered through. "I'm Julian," he said. "Julian Capulet."

Rome glanced up shyly. He noticed a bright splash of yellow across Julian's forefingers. It seemed to grow and take over his whole view. "What needed yellow?" Rome asked.

"Hm?" Julian replied, clearly puzzled. Then he followed Rome's eyes to his hands. "I was just doing a little painting. Guess I didn't wash it all off."

Rome grinned, picturing Julian with a paintbrush behind his ear. Too cute!

"I'd love to see your art one day," Rome said. He cautiously put his own hand on the edge of his side of the shelf. He pushed it slowly toward Julian's. A tingling sensation ran through his fingertips as they softly brushed against each other. It was like he'd connected a circuit. The air was charged, like just before a rainfall.

Rome felt sweat begin to drip down the back of

his neck. This was too much. What were the chances of running into this guy twice? It had to be fate.

He leaned into the tiny space between the books. There was just enough room for them to whisper. "Would you mind if I tested something?" he asked quietly.

Julian simply nodded.

Rome confessed, "I sort of haven't really — I haven't felt the way I felt when we . . ." He paused, trying to find the words. "I guess, I want to be sure."

Julian moved forward, pushing a few books off the shelf along the way. He pressed his lips against Rome's. The tingling between them became an all-out electrical storm. Rome let himself get swept away.

"Hey, you two!" called the shopkeeper from the front. "Not *in* the books, would ya?"

"Hey, is that you, Julian? Who you got there?" another voice called out. Footfalls came from the back. Someone was coming to see what was happening.

Julian looked away and Rome began breathing rapidly. His heart was pounding in his chest.

Was this real? Was this really happening? Rome began to panic. He was in a gay bookstore, with a gay boy, who he had been kissing and wanted to kiss again. And more gay people were coming to talk to them about things he could only assume would also be gay.

*I don't want to just run away again*, he thought. But he had to get out of there. Rome shot a nervous look to Julian. Amazingly, the other boy seemed to understand.

The two moved quickly to the end of the shelf. They ran out of The Orchard, hand in hand.

# 07 *Getting Real*

THE SUN WAS SETTING AS JULIAN pulled Rome along the bustling Osborne Street strip. They raced by busy bars, loud music, neon signs. Turning sharply, they worked their way through the park outside the government buildings, and then beyond into the downtown core. They passed a couple of places with big rainbow signs. Rome thought they must be straight-up (or gay-up?) sex clubs.

He marvelled at how nice it felt to hold

someone's hand. Julian's grip was soft and strong, all at once. *If Ben, or even Marty, saw me right now, I'd never live it down*, Rome thought. But he didn't let go.

The Hungry Rhino sat in the centre of the Exchange District. It was marked by an overhanging sign in the shape of a rhinoceros.

Julian brought Rome to a table near the back, pointing out the menu scrawled on the wall in chalk. "This is one of my favourite restaurants!" Julian burst out. Once the silence was broken, he started talking fast, going on about the food, the commune-style staff system at the restaurant, and half-a-million other things Rome didn't quite catch.

Rome looked over the menu. Everything seemed to be organic, local, and full-on vegetarian. He narrowed his eyes at a food option titled the "B"LT. Fiddling with his class ring, Rome realized that this area seemed to live up to all the horror stories his parents had warned him about. *Sex clubs, communists, fake meats? What have I gotten myself into?*

Rome glanced up and took in Julian for a moment. This all felt surreal, like sitting down to dinner with a daydream. He looked at Julian's hand on the table and had an impulse to just reach out and take it. But he pulled back, unsure. Rome traced his fingers around the edge of his class ring and then down to the scar on his left hand, wondering what he could say.

Finally, Julian said, "Well, I'm gonna get the tofu strips. Want me to order for both of us?"

Rome nodded. "Sure. I'll have, uh, whatever you think is good."

Rome peeked at Julian's backside as he walked away. *Damn*, he thought. Then he looked down, blushing, feeling sinful.

After ordering, Julian hopped back into his seat and looked at Rome expectantly.

*I might as well just go for it*, Rome figured. But where to start? He didn't want to give Julian the wrong impression. But what was the right one anyway? Rome shook his head, tired of getting stuck in his thoughts. "I'm not exactly . . . out," he said at last. Julian seemed to understand, and, just like that, Rome felt lighter.

He decided it would be easier to focus the conversation on Julian. He asked him question after question. When did he figure himself out? How did it go with his parents? And what about at school? With every answer, Rome found he could listen and respond easily, exploring every little tangent. As he found out more about Julian, Rome only became more excited to get to know him better.

Julian really seemed to come from another world. His mom was bisexual. What kind of luck was that! Plus, his cousin was a guy who liked dating guys, too. Clearly, Julian had never had to worry about 'coming out' or weirdness like that. "That's so cool," Rome said, with a hint of jealousy. But his envy melted when he learned about Julian's high-school years.

"I just could never really fit in." Julian dipped his tofu strips into some sweet brown sauce. "With a mom like mine, I never had a chance!" He said the words with a laugh, but they didn't sound very funny.

"So what'd you do?" Rome asked. He cautiously picked at his own meal. It definitely didn't look like real meat. But, then, he wasn't sure what he had been expecting.

"Tried to hang back, mostly," Julian replied. He wasn't looking Rome in the eye anymore. "Mom — she's always been the type to step out and face any big fight. Honestly, sometimes it can be a bit much." Julian studied the table. "I tried to balance her out, I guess. I'm not really the fighter type. Not like her."

"What about your cousin?" Rome asked. "You said he's . . . well, is he like your mom, too? Front of the fight and all that?"

Julian shrugged. "I don't know. Not really, I don't think. He wasn't when I knew him. But it's been a while. We haven't really talked much since he got out of corrections."

Rome wasn't sure what to say to that, so he changed the subject. "So, uh, you're done school now?"

Julian shrugged. "Well . . . I kinda . . . dropped out."

Rome's eyes went wide. "But, Julian, you're so smart!"

"It's not like I wanted to," Julian replied. His voice was a little stern. Then he sighed, softening again. He looked back at Rome at last. "I just couldn't take it anymore. People used to say all kinds of shit about me, about my mom, and . . . well, anyway, they didn't make it easy for me."

Rome bit his lip. "I'm sorry."

"It happens," Julian answered. "I'm doing online stuff now, trying to get my last credit."

Rome nodded. "Wow . . . even after all that, you're still trying to finish. That's pretty cool. Kinda really brave, actually." He shrugged. "I don't know what I'd do if I had to deal with half that stuff."

"You're about to graduate, right?" Julian asked. "You never had any trouble?"

Rome shook his head. "It's been all right. Being on the team helps a lot." He motioned to the flaming basketball emblazoned on his jacket. "No shortage of friends."

"Sounds like a dream." Julian raised an eyebrow. Rome couldn't tell if he was being sarcastic.

"I guess . . ." With a sigh, Rome admitted, "I mean, no one gives me trouble, so long as I don't let them down." Looking around the restaurant, at all the weird looking people and funky food, he felt a little jealous again. "Sometimes, it makes it hard. I just want so bad to be normal, to do all the stuff people expect of me. But I gotta wonder, what it would be like if I could just be . . . me, you know? God, that's cheesy. I'm sorry."

"No," Julian replied. He rested his hand on Rome's. "That's real."

Talk with Julian flowed easily. They even navigated over the rocky bits. Julian knew so much about everything. It was like being on a date with a dictionary. *But, like, a sexy dictionary*, thought Rome with a bit of a smirk.

Being with Julian was cool, like hanging out with a friend and going on a date at the same time.

It reminded Rome a bit of being with Rosie, back when they would hang for hours on end and just talk, goofing around enough that he could really let his walls down and just be, without overthinking it. Of course, with Rosie, there was the weirdness that she was a girl, and so everyone figured they were dating. Meanwhile, the weirdness with Julian was that he wasn't a girl. And yet Rome couldn't take his eyes off him.

After Rome picked up the bill, they stepped outside. It was cooler now, and Julian asked if they could snuggle for warmth. Rome welcomed him closer, wrapping his jacket around the two of them. He was sore at the very thought of letting go. "I guess this is goodbye?"

Julian asked, with a timid grin, "Why don't you just come over to my place?"

# 08 Weird and Wonderful

ROME FOLLOWED THE TWISTING colours as they traced the outline of a city, spattered with bright lights and swirling stars above, a moon on one side and a sun on the other. Rome turned to Julian in amazement. "Did you make that?"

"Mostly it was my mom," Julian replied, shrugging, as if the incredible mural on the side of his house was nothing special. He opened the front door and stepped inside. Inhaling sharply, Rome glanced over the painting one more time before pushing himself across the threshold.

The house was old, full of what some might lovingly call character. A voice in Rome's mind, which sounded oddly like his mother's, started criticizing the place, but he pushed away those thoughts. He tried to keep an open mind as he took in the scuff marks on the hardwood floor and dents in the walls. All the furniture seemed to be different colours and styles, a few held together with duct tape or stitches. There were shelves leaning heavy with jars of herbs and preserves. On the walls there were more murals, like the one outside. Some of them stretched up to the ceilings, filled with rainbows, pentacles, dancing naked bodies. Julian had said his mom was . . . different.

"Is that my boy?!" a booming voice called out.

"Mom! You're home!" Julian shouted with joy as he ran forward to be scooped up into a hug.

*This is his mom?* Rome raised his eyebrows. The woman was loud, bright, and had a frame that took up much of the hallway. She had a broad smile that lit up, along with her sparkling eyes, as she lifted her son into the air and squeezed him joyfully. Her bright violet hair had salt-and-pepper roots poking through, and was cut so short Rome might have mistaken her for a man if he saw her from behind. In comparison, Julian seemed small, muted, and even frail.

As the woman let Julian go, her sharp eyes glanced Rome over just a moment. Julian stepped back, motioning to Rome. "Mom, this is Romeo," he said. "I'm having him over tonight." Rome blushed and quickly looked down at his shoes. Hearing Julian call him 'Romeo' felt intimate, like a touch on the back of his neck. Remembering his manners, Rome gave a polite wave to Julian's mother. She gave a curt nod in response.

Rome followed the pair deeper into the strange house. Julian and his mother caught up, and Rome began to notice their similarities — the way they both talked with their hands, the similar intonation in their voices. They even had the same dimples when they smiled! The more he watched, the more alike they became.

Rome had so much he wanted to know. What was it like to be bi, and be a mom? He'd never even heard of that being possible! Did she really date girls and guys? Did she ever do it at the same time? Did she try to bring them home? Rome burned with questions, but there didn't seem to be any right time to ask anything. Julian and his mother were already talking back and forth, not even pausing as she leaned over to pull something from the oven.

Julian reached out, grabbing at the food. His mother pulled the tray of brownies away before he could sneak a bite. "These are hot!" she warned. "Besides, they're not for you. Not unless you plan on showing up tomorrow night. We've got a lot to do before Saturday. We're doing another demo, this time even bigger! We could really use you at the planning meeting."

*A demo?* Even more questions came to Rome. *Like a demolition? Or maybe a demonstration? But of what?*

"We'll see," replied Julian. He was clearly not that enthused.

His mother laughed and prodded him. "I'll get you one of these days — you'll see. By the time you're my age, you'll be the one bringing on the revolution, while I put my feet up at home!"

Rome's eyes went wide. Julian really hadn't been kidding. His mom was something else! It was kind of scary, but also kind of cool.

Julian's mother glanced at Rome for just a moment again. Then she gestured at the dishes in the sink. "Now, Jules, would you and your friend be dears and wash these for me?"

Julian passed a cloth in Rome's direction. Rome guessed he was being put on drying duty. With a short lull in the conversation, Rome figured now was as good a time as any to jump in. "It's nice to meet you, Mrs. Capulet," he said politely.

"Is it?" the woman replied, as she pulled off her oven mitts. Rome shot a nervous look at Julian. Had he said something wrong already?

After letting Rome worry for a bit, Julian's mother relented. "You can call me Angie. Angie Liang."

"Uh, okay, Angie," Rome said. He felt a bit weird calling a parent by a first name. But it was clear by now that Angie wasn't like most parents he knew. And he liked that about her.

Angie was different, there was no doubt. She was funny, for starters, and acted more like a friend than a mom. Though Rome could see she had no problem putting Julian in his place when she had to. It was cool to watch them interact. Rome could see little bits of Julian poking through Angie. Or was it the other way around?

Once the dishes were done, Julian led Rome up to his bedroom. *I can't believe his mom just lets him bring guys home to sleep over!* How awesome was that?

On their way upstairs, Julian's mom called behind them, "You know where the condom jar is!"

Romeo felt a bolt of shock as he processed what Angie had said. "The condom jar?" he whispered to Julian.

"Mom's a very sex-positive feminist," Julian replied, as if this was something that required no more explanation.

The door to Julian's bedroom matched the rest of the house. It was covered with drawings, stickers, and posters. But inside, the art that covered Julian's room had its own distinct style. Rome looked around and took in the canvases stacked everywhere. A few were still on easels, more on the floor, others peeking out from under clothes, or stacked in the closet. All were covered in colours that flowed and burst out, a medley of waterfalls and supernovas. Looking around in awe, Rome announced, "This is wonderful."

# 09 Stories and Scars

A SHIVER RAN THROUGH ROME'S BODY. Julian was close to him now, and they were finally, really, alone. *What happens now?* Rome wondered.

Once they had the courage to touch, it was only moments before they were running their hands over each other. Rome was breathing heavily. More shivers ran up his spine as his fingertips traced Julian's jawline.

When it got to be too much, both found that words came easily and helped bring down the tension.

Julian told Rome about everything from colour gradients to the reason the sky was blue. Rome was sure he could listen to that voice forever.

"So, what did Angie mean?" asked Rome. "All that talk about 'demos' and 'revolution'?"

Julian chuckled. "That's her politics. She's always got some new project on the go." His voice was distant. "She tries to get me involved but . . . I don't know . . ."

"You don't want to save the world?" Rome asked with a smile. Julian didn't answer. "Hey," Rome said, gently squeezing Julian's hand. "I was just kidding."

"I know. It's just . . . It can be a lot of pressure, being her kid. I don't know if I could ever do everything she's able to do." Julian sighed, pulling his fingers through Rome's hair. "I don't want to let her down. I really want to do the right thing . . . But I just don't know if I can."

"I get that," Rome replied. He ran his hand along Julian's side. "Well, sort of. I mean, my folks expect a lot of me, too. Everybody does, really. The team, my teachers, even guys like Marty and Ben. But sometimes, I don't think they get me at all, not really. All they see is what they want to see." He sighed, rubbing the scar on his left hand. "Sometimes it feels like I'm just made of secrets."

Julian's eyes followed Rome's fingers along the mark. "How'd you get that?"

Rome bit his lip. He'd never told anyone that story — not seriously, anyway. Sometimes he'd joke about it with Marty and Ben. Most people didn't ask. *But*, he thought, *Julian's not most people.*

"We don't have to talk about it," Julian said, pulling back.

Rome offered his palm to Julian, showing him the complete line. "My dad can be kind of a scary guy."

Julian reached out to trace along the scar's edge. Rome shuddered. He'd never let anyone touch it like that before. "Did he do this to you?" Julian asked softly.

"Not exactly," Rome sighed. He closed his eyes and rolled to rest his head on Julian's lap. "I mean, I don't even really remember. He was just upset about, I don't know, something. There was a lot of shouting, and something broke. A plate, I think? Somehow, my hand got cut."

"Was your mom there?" Julian asked.

Rome nodded. "Yeah, she was just . . . cold. Like, quiet. Didn't say a word to him. Or to me." As the memory came back, Rome gulped. He didn't want to cry in front of Julian. "I just ran away."

Julian's fingers fell back into Rome's hair. Rome figured he might as well finish the story. "God, I haven't thought about it in a while. I was, maybe twelve? Not even? We had just moved to the neighbourhood. And so, after it happened, I ran off. Made it out to one of those little lakes around there, near the golf course. Marty and Ben were there, playing around. That's kinda how we met." Rome chuckled. "All I wanted to do was goof around with them, even though I was all bloody and shit!" He looked up to see Julian listening intently.

"They tried to help," Rome explained. "Ben said we could live out there for days if we had to. Marty tried to act like he knew how to take care of a cut.

And I just hid out there for hours. When I got back, my mom saw me all muddy, and she just flipped! Got me a phone that year, too. She swore she'd never lose track of me again . . ." He trailed off. He hadn't called her yet to check in.

Julian took Rome's hand and gently kissed the scar. "I'm sorry that happened, Romeo."

Rome flushed. "It's kind of cool. Marty and Ben and me, we've been friends ever since. Must have been fate, right? Besides, my dad hasn't been like that since then, either. I think Mom made him go to counselling or something. We never really talk about it. Now, whenever shit gets tense, they just drink until they calm down."

Julian was quiet for a while. Rome was starting to have second thoughts about sharing that story when, finally, Julian stood up. He moved to turn off the light.

Julian's voice was distant again as he started to undo his jeans. "You shared your scars with me."

Rome's mind began to race and his hands started to shake. "I've never . . ."

When Julian exposed his upper thigh, Rome realized there were thin scars along his leg and one long gash, like a lighting strike. Julian didn't look up as he took Rome's hand and placed it on his thigh. Rome ran his fingers over the raised skin.

Julian told Rome his story — the bullying at school, the long, lonely nights, the pain it took to just keep going. Julian cut himself to stay alive. And then he cut again and again, when he felt like he couldn't keep going anymore. "I just wanted to die," Julian whispered.

Rome wasn't sure what to say. He'd heard about people cutting, but this was Julian. He didn't want to think of Julian hurting that bad. But it wasn't like Rome was a stranger to self-harm. When things got to be too much, he turned to smoking and drinking to feel that burning rush, basking in the emptiness that followed. Just like his parents. Rome pulled Julian back down to the bed and held him. His arms wrapped around the Julian's soft stomach, Rome breathed into his hair, "I'm glad you kept going. I'm glad you're here now."

"Okay! Okay!" Rome relented. He couldn't concentrate enough to fight both his mother and Julian. "I'll be home for dinner! God!"

Rome could practically hear his mother stiffen. She hated it when he 'used the Lord's name in vain.' Her reply was sharp. "All right. Dinner, then."

"I'll talk to you later." Rome moved to hang up.

"And?" she asked expectantly. "Isn't there something you want to say to me?"

"Mom," he grumbled.

"I love you, Romeo."

"Yeah of course," he answered. "You too." Still, he knew that wasn't enough. She would make him say it before she let him off the hook.

"You what?" she asked.

"I don't want to say it. I'm in front of the guys!" Rome felt himself turning red. He saw Julian suppress a giggle.

"What if this is the last time I speak to you, Romeo? I could be dead before you even get home. Or you could —"

"Okay, okay!" Rome relented. "I love you too! Goodbye!" He ended the call before she could get in another word, just as Julian broke out laughing. "Oh my God!" Rome shouted as he pushed Julian off with a grin.

Angie didn't seem to be around, so they had the house to themselves. Julian whipped up some pancakes while Rome tried to help by setting the table. Everything was mismatched — the plates, the cups, even the knives and forks. The whole house was like a big art project, with Julian at the centre.

Rome snuck up behind Julian, who was focused on flipping the pancakes. He slipped his arms around Julian's waist. Julian kissed Rome's cheek and inhaled deeply, murmuring something about breakfast. *I thought this would be weird*, thought Rome, helping Julian carry the food to the table. *But it's the most normal I've ever felt.*

The sun shone brightly as they went out for an afternoon wander. The warm day hinted at the beginning of a hot summer. Rome looked around at the potholes in the street, the worn-down porches, the random-looking tags on the walls. *If Marty and Ben were here*, Rome thought, *they'd call this place sketchy*.

In Rome's neighbourhood, it was all perfect lawns and manicured parks. All his neighbours' dirty secrets were firmly kept behind the blank front doors. Rome shook his head and tried to see the place through Julian's eyes instead.

Families were out on their stoops. Kids played on the sidewalk. Stray cats sprawled out in the sunlight.

"I think it's beautiful here," said Rome. And he meant it.

They stopped to look at the community garden Julian's mom had helped start. An older woman lifted her sunhat and said hello to them. Rome noticed she talked to Julian like he was family. Julian seemed to fit in around here but, still, Rome felt a shudder up his back when he thought about the two of them being seen together in public. When he noticed a few passers-by giving them side-glances, Rome's palms began to sweat.

He knew, ironically, it was just a couple days ago that he would have been the one giving weird looks — or worse. The face of the man who kicked him out of Rose and Lyla's party flashed in his mind. For all Rome had told Julian, he hadn't raised that topic yet. *I'll bring it up when the time is right*, Rome told himself.

Rome and Julian grabbed food at a diner over on the main street, picking a seat by the window where they could watch people go by. The pair never ran out of things to say to each other. Finally, as the sun sank low in the sky, turning the world pink and gold, Rome knew he had to go.

The couple worked their way back toward Julian's home. Rome studied Julian, blushing as he thought, *He's so incredible*. Rome squeezed Julian's hand. *He just makes me feel so . . .*

Before he could finish the thought, a passing car jumped into view. It veered toward them at a frightening pace. It skidded just next to the curb, making Rome jump. For a moment, Rome's heart raced as he thought maybe the car had lost control. Then he heard what the guys inside the car were shouting. "Eat my ass, homos!"

Without another thought, Rome took off running. He pulled Julian along with him. Rome couldn't stop, couldn't listen, couldn't do anything until he and Julian were safe. In his mind, a thought played on repeat: *What if that's someone I know?!*

When they finally stopped Rome's hands were sweating. His head was pounding. He knew Julian was trying to calm him down, but the shame wouldn't go away. Finally, he smacked his head, shouting, "I'm so stupid!"

"What? Why?" Julian asked, concern in his voice.

Rome's heart felt like a heavy stone. He tried to answer, but the words escaped him.

After a long silence, Julian looked down, dejected. "I'm sorry."

"No," said Rome, reaching out to him. "It's my fault." The thought that Julian blamed himself gave

Rome the will to speak. "It's just that . . . that used to be me. Pretty recently," he confessed.

Julian pulled away and Rome felt an ache in his chest. He hung his head and stood, saying, "I should go."

"So that's it?" Julian asked.

The hurt in Julian's eyes broke Rome's heart. This couldn't be it — this couldn't be the end! Rome shook his head, fighting off tears. "I'll be back. I promise."

Rome's heart pounded all the way back to his suburban home on the south side of town. All he could think was that he wished he was still with Julian. The houses and side streets that he'd always taken for granted now seemed unfamiliar. His clothes felt too tight and he pulled at his collar, trying to get a breath of fresh air. Sweat was building on his palms and the back of his neck.

When Rome got home he hurried past his mother. She clearly had something on the tip of her tongue. He'd missed dinner.

Rome curled up in his room, his trusty pop-bottle whiskey by his side. He shot a text to Rose, thanking her for brunch. Then he sent one to Julian, letting him know he'd arrived home, safe and sound. Late into the night, Rome kept his cell close. His heart raced every time he got a text back from either of them. Between messages, he started to search the corners of the internet. He was abuzz with curiosity after such an incredible couple of days. Finally, in the wee hours of the morning, he fell into a restless sleep, phone still in hand.

# 11 *Confession*

ROME RUBBED HIS EYES on the way to school.
Bad dreams still clung to the edges of his mind.
Sensing something behind him, Rome glanced over
his shoulder. Nothing was there. Just the same old
houses, the same old trees, the same old sidewalks, and
big open sky. "Shake it off," he told himself. But the
feeling wouldn't leave.

It was only a matter of time until his friends found
out — about him, about Julian. Rome shuddered.

If he told Marty, Ben would know for sure. And if Ben knew, he'd probably tell the whole team. And if the team knew . . . It seemed like a never-ending downward spiral. Pretty soon, the whole school would hear. Word would spread to even the teachers. And then his parents. What would his mom say? God, what would his dad do?

Rome's stomach grumbled. He decided he needed a smoke. He rifled through his bag and found the few stray cigarettes he kept in an old mint tin, nestled with a small lighter. He lit one up before hurrying off to first period.

Rome could barely pay attention in class. He mulled over what Lyla had said about what to do not *if* someone found out, but *when*. Maybe he should try to get ahead of this whole thing. Or at least tell someone. It was starting to feel like it might burst out of him anyway.

Scary as it was, he was excited! He'd spent so many years playing at romance with Rosie, letting everybody believe they were in love. Now that he had really found someone, he wanted to tell everyone! Rome bit his lip, trying to hold himself back from shouting it out in the halls.

On his morning spare, Rome ducked into the guidance counsellor's office. He had been in a few times over the years. Sometimes it was after getting in trouble. More often it was to just talk about stuff going on with the team or at school.

The guidance counsellor, Lawrence, was the kind of teacher who let you call him by his first name. He sported a silver cross hanging by a ring from his ear and told stories about the ska band he had 'back in the day.' There'd even been rumours that he was gay, since he was always referring to his 'partner' Alex. Of course, that rumour stopped when Lawrence announced Alex was pregnant. *Though Lawrence could still be bi or something*, Rome mused, trying to think like Julian, *or Alex could be transgender*. But the best thing about Lawrence, by far, was that you could really trust him — once that door was closed, that was it.

The door was unlocked, but Lawrence wasn't inside. Rome settled into one of the comfy beige chairs and looked around at the room. The space was filled with photos of graduates, letters of thanks, and books like *Learning to Learn*, *Chicken Stew for the Musical Soul*, and *50 Ways to Transform that Anger into Productivity*. Rome chuckled a little at the cheesy titles, then turned to the wall of pamphlets behind the desk. They advertised help for what seemed like any problem, from *Chlamydia is Not a Flower*, to *Ask Before Opening: Learning Good Consent*. Rome even noticed a pamphlet that looked just like the one Lyla had given him!

"Well, hey there!" Lawrence appeared in the doorway. He wore a big smile, and took a long sip from his massive travel mug before taking a seat behind the desk.

"Hey, Lawrence. I need some advice. And, like, somewhere just to chill. That cool?" Rome asked, chewing at his lip. The worries were starting to creep back into his head.

"Cool as a cucumber," Lawrence answered in a sing-song voice. "What's on your mind, bud?" he asked, leaning in. Already he had that look that he got when getting ready for some top-notch listening.

Rome glanced away. Suddenly, he felt not quite up to eye contact. "Um . . . I guess I — It's just that . . ." Rome shut his eyes. "I think I'm falling in love!"

It wasn't exactly what he was planning to say, but there it was. Rome cautiously opened one eye, trying to read Lawrence's reaction.

"Okay." Lawrence nodded and took another long sip. "You seem upset for someone in love. Are you and Rosie having problems?"

Rome laughed. Of course! Everyone at school still thought he and Rosie were an item. "No, no, she's with someone else now. Someone she met in university." Rome waved his hand in the air, as if to fan the very thought of that away. Before Lawrence could ask, Rome added, "I met someone new, too."

Lawrence nodded sagely. "Mhm. Well, tell me about this new girl."

Thinking of Julian, Rome felt himself blush. "Well, we're really different. But it's cool. Like, that's what makes it work? We have so much to talk about! And even though we just met I can't stop thinking about him —" Rome froze, realizing he'd just let it slip. He looked up, but Lawrence didn't seem to have noticed. Rome said it again. "Yeah, he's like, the most amazing person I've ever met."

"Well," Lawrence chuckled, "it sounds like you're over Rosie!"

Rome shrugged. Now that it was out there, he couldn't think of anything else to say. He waited for a reaction, for something to change. But things didn't feel different. He had told someone about Julian, and the world hadn't ended. He was still sitting there in the same office, looking at the same man he'd known for years. It all felt so normal! And, to his surprise, that kind of bothered him. At least when he'd told Rose and Lyla, they had been excited. But Lawrence simply sat there.

Rome crossed his arms. Shouldn't he be surprised? Did he just not care? Or, maybe he didn't hear Rome right. Rome's eyes grew wide as an even more disturbing thought came to him. *Oh God, has he been able to tell all along?*

Rome's palms were getting sweaty again. He began to fiddle with his ring. Finally, he tried to say it, clear as day. "I think, maybe I'm, uh, gay?"

Lawrence simply nodded, so Rome decided to keep going. "I told Rosie — um, Rose, I mean. She's actually a lesbian now, or I guess she always was? Anyway, she just moved in with this chick, Lyla, who's pretty cool too." Lawrence's expression didn't change. There was still just that placid smile. "And this guy, Julian . . ." Rome trailed off. He felt his face turn warm again. "He's, um, really nice . . ."

Once Rome started describing Julian, he found he couldn't stop. Finally, once Rome had run out of words completely, Lawrence spoke up. "That's really rad, Rome!"

Rome just shrugged. "I mean, I guess."

Lawrence took another long sip before announcing, "You know, I think I have just the pamphlet for this!" He put down the mug and started rummaging through his supplies.

"Uh, I don't really need that," Rome replied. "But, I was sorta hoping you could help me out with something else. I kind of want to tell the guys about this, um, new thing. Maybe? I mean, I don't know. I don't know how to not say something. But how do I even . . . ?"

Lawrence looked up, eyes sparkling. "Would you like me to page them into the office? We could all have a nice chat. I think I have some tea." He moved to another section of his desk, pulling out various boxes of green, black, and herbal teas.

"Er — I, don't, uh . . ." Rome tried to find his words. Having Ben and Marty paged so he could tell them he was gay was the most awkward thing he could imagine.

Lawrence sat back up. "All right." He went to his rack of books and pulled something out. "You could let them read this!" He passed over a small booklet titled, *Man Up for your Man Friends who like Men: The Straight but Not Narrow Project.*

Rome squirmed a little. The uneasy feeling was in his stomach again. With a polite thanks to Lawrence, Rome took the reading material. He said a quick goodbye before he went off, hoping to grab a snack before his next class.

# 12 *Trouble*

AS THE TEACHER DRONED ON in afternoon English, Rome zoned out. His thoughts flitted from his feelings for Julian, to worries over what his friends were going to say, to concerns over his parents. And all those damn pamphlets! Telling Lawrence had just made things feel more confusing, and the pressure was building up inside him again. Nervously, Rome texted Marty and Ben under the desk, suggesting they meet up after school. They agreed, of course, with Marty suggesting they go to his place. His parents were away for work again, off to Berlin this time for a conference or something.

By the end of the day, Rome was dragging his feet as he headed toward the school doors. Maybe he shouldn't say anything. Or maybe he should tell them right away? *Oh God, there they are*, he thought.

Ben and Marty were smoking at the edge of the parking lot. Just as Rome was about to open the door and call out to them, something else grabbed their attention. Rome saw a massive truck pull up. Once he stepped outside, he could hear Ben shouting at the two beefy guys coming out of the vehicle.

"Hey, homos!" Ben threw his smoke to the ground, sending sparks flying into a patch of weeds. "You wanna start something?" he asked with a laugh. "Or you get lost looking for a place to suck cock?"

Rome recognized the bigger of the two guys as the one who'd kicked him out of Rose and Lyla's party. *This is gonna be trouble*, thought Rome, heading toward the commotion. He saw Ben already getting riled up, while Marty still hung back.

Heat seemed to rise off the asphalt of the parking lot as tensions grew. Ben and the taller of the two bald men approached each other, while Ben hurled out insults. The big, buff guy flexed a little, pushing against his shirt, forcing Ben to notice their size difference. As he got closer, Rome could see Marty was sweating heavily and nervously watching the school doors. Marty glanced toward Rome, as if asking him to do something. Rome looked back, unsure if he wanted to see a teacher peeking out or not.

Before Rome could even reach the action, the other guy, who seemed to be the bigger one's boyfriend, came up and patted his partner on the back. Thankfully, the gesture seemed to be enough. The pair turned to leave. Rome let out a short sigh of relief. *That could have been worse.*

As they made their way back to the truck, Marty seemed to find his nerve. "Yeah, you better run!" Marty shouted, puffing up his chest. He only stuttered a little as he called after the couple. "F-Faggots!"

Rome froze. The guys were almost inside their truck. He sent out a silent prayer that they would just leave. *Just go home. Please.*

The bigger of the pair looked over his shoulder at Marty, who now seemed a lot less sure of himself. The man slowly walked right up to Marty, looking him up and down, his face unreadable. Finally, he cocked an eyebrow and loudly asked, "Who you kidding, Mary?" Marty's jaw dropped as the stranger added, "You're not fooling anyone."

A deep red ran across Marty's cheeks. That's when he let the first punch fly.

Marty's fist connected with the man's jaw at an odd angle, making Marty shout in surprise. Rome began to run toward the group, calling to Marty, "Dude, don't!"

The other buff guy ran back, coming to the aid of his partner. Ben got in the way, taking a shot at the first guy's side. The stranger was tough, but he didn't expect Ben's hit. He reeled back.

As Rome rushed over, the bigger guy pushed him back and knocked him to the ground. Then he swung back at Marty, hitting him right in the teeth. His fist collided with Marty's braces. Both of them yowled as the buff guy's hand was cut by the metal in Marty's mouth. Blood burst from the inside of Marty's lip.

Something clicked inside Rome. No longer thinking, he stood and ran forward. He was furious, frustrated, tired of this whole thing. With a full-on body slam, Rome tackled the taller stranger to the ground. They were only down for a moment before he was pulled off by the second guy, who threw Rome to the side like a heavy gym bag.

Then Ben pulled out his phone. "You goddamn animals!" he screamed. "One more move and I'm calling the cops!"

The two men shared a look. They leaped into the truck and took off, speeding into the street. Ben shouted swears and empty threats after them. Rome got up and tried to help Marty with his busted-up lip.

Lawrence's voice rang out from across the parking lot. In seconds, he was at the side of the three young men. He was followed by the steady footsteps of the vice principal, Mrs. Duke.

Marty was taken to the hospital to get checked out. Rome and Ben were escorted inside and taken to the main office.

"I hope they call the cops on those fudge-packers," Ben growled. His hands were still balled into fists. "We should get a damn medal, keeping this place safe from pervos like that. I bet we could sue those guys! Oh, just wait until my step-dad hears about this!"

While Ben went on, Rome just sighed. He looked down at his hands, wiping off the bits of rock stuck in his palm. That certainly hadn't gone the way he wanted.

"Romeo Montague," the secretary called out, "your parents should be here in a few minutes."

"Well, crap," Rome said under his breath.

# 13 Breaking Point

"MARTY?! IN THE TEETH?!" Rome's father bellowed. His face was turning red. "You got the guy back, right?!"

Rome's mother stayed silent. She frowned as she stared at the vice principal's nameplate on the dark wooden desk.

Mrs. Duke looked at the whole Montague family as if she couldn't believe what she was hearing. "Mr. and Mrs. Montague, I hope you realize how seriously we need to take this incident." Her tone was level and icy. "Your son took part in a violent assault while he was on school property. This is grounds for automatic suspension, if not expulsion."

Rome felt numb. The details of what happened were all blurring together. Did he really do that? Was that really him? It felt like he'd been in Mrs. Duke's office for ages, watching his parents and the vice principal going back and forth. Glancing up at the clock, Rome sighed. It had only been about five minutes.

Finally, his mother spoke. "How did all of this start, Romeo? Was this a mean kid from school? A bully? Was he from some other sports team?" She extended a hand to place it on Rome's shoulder. His father pushed the hand away. "Don't smother the boy," he growled.

To Rome it all felt unreal. He wondered if he could have made a different decision. Maybe get involved sooner, or try to talk Ben and Marty down. It felt frustratingly simple, like he should be able to just retrace his steps and make it better. "We . . ." Words came to Rome, but slowly, as if they were floating up from somewhere very far away. Or perhaps he was floating. Yes, that was it, he felt like he was floating above himself, watching this all happen. That made it a little easier.

"We knew the guy. I mean, sort of. We'd seen him around." Rome ran his fingers in circles around the top of his class ring. "He pulled up, started saying stuff to Ben, I didn't really hear. And he, uh, he was with —" As Rome stumbled over his words, his father groaned in frustration. "We saw him with some other guy. Like, a boyfriend, or whatever." He didn't want to rat on his friends, or dig himself any deeper. At that point, he just went silent.

Rome's father's eyes grew wide. "Marty got beat up by a couple of gays?!" Rome couldn't tell if his father was upset or amused.

"I mean, he didn't get . . . beat. Just punched," Rome tried to explain.

His father was beet red at this point. His mother was looking away. Mrs. Duke turned up her nose, and Lawrence gave Rome a pitying look that made him feel even worse. *I'm gonna get kicked out of school for being a gay gay-basher*, Rome thought. "Jesus H. Christ," he muttered.

"Well, at least you sent those guys running," his father began. Mrs. Duke coughed and looked at him with disapproval. "I mean, uh, you're in big trouble, young man. This is obviously unacceptable behaviour."

Rome's stomach turned. He just kept his eyes down, studying his scar, trying to avoid his father's gaze.

Rome's mother chimed in. "Mrs. Duke, I'm sure you can agree this is hardly grounds for expulsion. Especially considering graduation is just a few weeks away." She was getting straight to the root of the problem, at least as she saw it — the risk of Rome failing to graduate. Rome wondered if she had any concern that her son might be a violent homophobe.

"Mrs. Montague," the vice principal replied, "Manitoba school divisions have a zero-tolerance policy regarding violence." Glaring at Rome, she went on. "In accordance with that policy, your son will be on a twenty-four-hour suspension. During this time, I will consult with the parents of the other students involved, the principal, and the superintendent. If we find that your son has had past incidents like this one, any vandalism or drug use, he is facing expulsion."

Rome's father just nodded. He was clearly growing tired of the conversation. Rome's mother went quiet, too, seemingly lost in thought. Mrs. Duke wasn't going to budge, that much was clear. Thankfully, the family was dismissed when Ben's step-father arrived and it became his turn to undergo the third-degree.

Heading to the door a step behind his parents, Rome felt a hand on his shoulder. Mrs. Duke leaned in, whispering to him directly. "Let me be clear. If I have any say in the matter, I will ensure you and your two friends do not graduate." Rome felt himself shaking as he followed his parents out the door.

Mrs. Duke called out to Mr. and Mrs. Montague, "Thank you for coming in on such short notice. I'll be in touch."

"God," Rome muttered to himself as he walked out of the school. He wondered if he'd ever even be let back inside.

Over dinner, Rome's part in the fight was the topic of endless discussion, mostly pronouncements spouted by his father. Pulling out his usual after-dinner drink early, Rome's father poured a glass of scotch. In turn, his mother pulled the cork out of a new bottle of wine, though in a far less festive mood. Both clearly felt the situation freed them from the need for the usual subtleties. Rome realized he was itching for a drink, too.

"They were probably high, stoned out of their gourd," said Rome's father. "Couple of pansies with nothing better to do than pick a fight with some high-school kids! Get a job! Am I right?" Rome's father mixed stereotypes like he was making a cocktail.

While his father got mouthier as he drank, Rome's mother turned sullen. She just quietly watched her son. Her blank expression was far more hurtful to Rome than any words his father could hurl.

Rome felt himself turning red and finally snapped, "Can you not? I just . . . Can I just be excused? Please?"

"You got a concussion or something?" His father grinned. "Come on, now, your first real fight! Of course, when they ask at school, make sure you tell them you've learned your lesson. You can say we beat you good for it!" As his father laughed, bits of food and spit flew through his teeth.

Rome's mother took a long sip of wine. "Those men were clearly troubled," she said, matter-of-factly. "You know, sometimes people need a wake-up call. Maybe God was working through you and your friends, helping put them on the right path." She reached out to tap his hand. "We will pray for them."

Rome pulled back and stood up from his seat. "Stop it!" he shouted.

"Calm down," his father replied at equal volume. "We're on your side!"

Rome shot him an angry look. Squeezing his fists, he said through clenched teeth, "No! You aren't! I wish it hadn't happened. I wish I'd never even —"

"You don't mean that," his mother interrupted. "Why, who knows what could have happened, they could have killed Marty. Or worse, ra —"

"Don't say it!" Rome couldn't let her finish the thought. "My God, don't even!"

Standing as well, his mother finally had a reaction. "We do not use the Lord's name in vain in this household."

Not to be outdone, his father stood too. But, with nothing to say, he just puffed up his shoulders and glared.

"Jesus!" Rome said, mostly to get under his mother's skin. He turned and headed out of the room. After grabbing his coat, he looked back at his parents. His mother's face was white with shock, his father's turning nearly purple. Rome saw his father reach for the dinner plate, and that was it. Rome was gone, out the door, not about to get another scar.

Rome could barely hear his father yelling after him as he stormed away. He slammed the door and hopped into his car. There was a buzzing in his stomach. He felt it inch up to his chest and fill his brain. Driving away, he felt giddy, almost high. Most amazingly, he didn't feel a trace of guilt. His mind focused on one thought, and one thought alone: *I have to go to Julian.*

# 14 Revelations

BY THE TIME ROME ARRIVED at Julian's, the buzz he had felt at running away had faded. It was replaced by shaky hands, worry sweats, and a heavy feeling in his stomach. "God, please, let him be home," Rome pleaded under his breath. He knocked, but there was no answer.

After a few minutes, he went back to the car to try to call Julian. As he rooted through his car he realized that in his rush to leave he'd forgotten the one thing that he actually needed — his phone!

He went back and knocked even louder. This time, a figure came to the door, and Rome's heart leaped in his chest. But something was wrong. Even once he opened the door, Julian didn't move to hug him or even smile.

"I heard what happened," said Julian, his voice flat, eyes stern.

Without a single hope left, Rome broke down. Tears began to roll down his cheeks, salty and hot. He was sorry. Sorry about the guy he'd hit, sorry about his parents, sorry he'd come to lay this all on Julian. He was exhausted, embarrassed, and out of options.

Julian pulled Rome inside and offered him a paint-stained rag to dry his tears. It took a while, but finally Rome caught his breath.

"How could you hurt someone like that?" Julian asked. "Did you really threaten to call the police?"

"I didn't know what to do," Rome tried to explain. "Honestly, I didn't even want to fight. When I got there, I was too late to stop it. And when

I saw him hit Marty I just lost it." Taking a deep breath, he tried to remember what had happened. "I think it was the blood — Marty's blood. It brought something out in me. I just . . . God, I wasn't thinking. I'm so sorry . . ."

"Romeo," Julian said at last. Rome blushed, just hearing the way Julian said his name. "That man you hurt, you'd seen him before, right? At the party?"

Rome nodded. He had to sit down as he remembered that night.

"The thing is," Julian said, staring at Rome, "that's Ty. My cousin."

Rome's heart began to race. That big, beefy guy was Julian's cousin?!

"The other guy is his partner, Harvey." Julian's voice faltered for the first time. "It's bad enough you — or, at least, your friends — started a fight with him. But threatening to call the police?" He shuddered. "Romeo, he could be sent back to prison. Or worse . . ."

Rome buried his face in his hands. *Why was this happening?*

Julian offered to call Ty to see if he would meet with Rome and try to talk things out. The thought was terrifying, scarier than the fight had been, for sure. But it was even scarier to think of losing Julian. So Rome agreed.

After more talking and some late-night coffee, Rome and Julian began to relax into each other's company again. Julian ran his fingers along Rome's scar as Rome told him about the fight with his parents. Something inside Rome quivered. Even though it was embarrassing for Rome to get so emotional, Julian really listened. That was special.

Rome was staring lovingly into Julian's eyes when there was a knock at the door.

"That must be Sami," said Julian, standing up. "I called them before you got here. Can you let them in? I'm gonna call Ty."

Rome nodded as he got up and went to answer the door, wondering, *Them?* He swung the door open to face down a single stranger. Had Julian been expecting more than one person?

"Hmmm . . . This is definitely Julian's house." The stranger stepped into the doorway with a giggle. "But you are definitely not Julian."

"Hey, Sami." Julian gave a quick wave from the kitchen.

Sami nodded, not looking away from Rome. "So you're the infamous Romeo." Sami smirked. "He's cute, I'll give you that. Not really my type, though."

"Sami, you don't have a type!" Julian laughed. "You barely have a preferred species!"

"I mean, I'm not gonna write off hooking up with an alien," Sami replied. They stepped inside and closed the door behind them.

Rome was dumbstruck, looking this stranger up and down. One moment, he was sure Sami was a girl, and then the next he wasn't so sure. Eventually, Rome just offered his hand, trying to be polite. This was Julian's friend after all. "Um, hey. Nobody really calls me that. Romeo, I mean. Just my mom. And Julian, I guess. But you can call me Rome?"

Sami accepted the handshake. "Hm, rough hands."

Rome wasn't sure what to say to that. Sami giggled again. "I'm just Sami, no more, no less. And you can use they and them as pronouns for me, thank-you-very-much."

Rome nodded, trying to piece it together. *Sami, they, Sami, they*, he tried to fix it in his mind. *Okay, I can get that. Sami, they, Sami, they* . . .

"Romeo, are you able to talk with Ty now? He says he can come over," Julian called out.

Rome felt a shiver run through his body. "Great, yeah."

Sami was . . . strange. But Rome was getting used to things being a bit upside-down when he was in Julian's world. Before long, the trio was sitting around the table, swapping stories about their parents.

"I know," Sami said, patting Rome's arm. "It can be pretty tough when your folks just don't get it." After a beat, they added, "Hell, it's hard enough to just be with myself half the time!"

Rome cracked up at that one. "No kidding! Man, sometimes it's like, I can just hear them in my head and —"

Before he could finish that thought, a knock came at the door. They all fell silent. Ty was there, and so was a heavy feeling in Rome's gut.

Ty came in with his partner and the group gathered in the living room. All five of them sat awkwardly for a minute or two as they tried to figure out how to proceed.

*Should I look him in the eye?* Rome wondered. *Shake his hand?* He began to chew at his lip. Should he laugh it off, or be serious? Should he wait for Ty to go first or start things by saying he was sorry?

Thankfully, Julian stepped in and got the ball rolling. After that, it was up to Rome to find the words.

"I'm really sorry," he said. "For today, for everything. It wasn't funny. It wasn't the kind of guy I want to be." After that, the words seemed to just flow out of him. He spoke the truth, all of it, tough as it might be to swallow. Ty nodded, listening quietly, holding Harvey's hand. Rome could see the cut on Ty's knuckles was still raw. Up close like that, the two guys, they seemed to Rome a lot less scary, and a lot more . . . real.

He was finally out of words, and the room settled

back into silence. Wringing his hands, Rome waited in suspense for a response.

Ty stood. He extended his hand to Rome. As Rome took Ty's hand, he felt himself pulled upwards and wrapped in a big bear hug. Rome patted Ty's back gently in thanks.

As Ty put Rome down, he said plainly, "You've got some shitty friends though, dude."

Rome nodded with a shrug — fair enough. After that, the conversation lightened, and soon the group felt like a bunch of friends just hanging out. At the end of the night, Sami caught a ride home with Ty and Harvey, leaving Rome and Julian alone in a house that felt warm with laughter.

Rome was in awe. *What kind of guy can do that?* he wondered. *Bring people together like that? And make it all look so easy.* Between the two of them, Julian was clearly the braver one. *I can't believe I get to be with him*, thought Rome as he followed up the creaking stairs to Julian's room.

Rome and Julian fell into bed together, laughing softly. They were both tired from the stress of the day.

But they found their energy again as soon as they were kissing. They became wrapped up in one another, in just the glow from a streetlight outside and a cloudy night sky above. Rome welcomed the darkness. He felt freer than he'd ever felt before. He pulled Julian's body against his own, giggling in joy and excitement.

Kisses moved along necklines, hands pulled, legs entwined. Even as they grew more passionate, Rome held back. He wasn't even sure how this was supposed to work, what was expected of him, what it was supposed to be like. Pushing through his nerves, he spoke up. "Wait, hold on a second."

"We don't have to," Julian said, backing off. "We can just —"

"No, I want to," Rome said, pulling Julian closer. "I do, it's just . . ." Rome looked Julian in the eyes and ran his fingers over Julian's back, caressing his warm skin. He felt something bubbling up, bursting to come out. He was tired of holding back. He wanted to be brave too. "Julian, I love you," Rome said.

# 15 Rock Bottom

THE SUN BROKE THROUGH the window and Rome's eyes fluttered open. He rolled over to find Julian curled up beside him. Rome took him into his arms and pulled him close, breathing deeply. Nothing would be the same, not after last night. And he wouldn't have it any other way. *I'm so gay*, thought Rome, with a smile.

Not wanting to wake Julian, Rome gently kissed his lover's cheek before gingerly pulling away.

Grabbing some scrap paper and a marker off the floor, he penned a quick message:

Gone to talk to parents. I'll call tonight.

Love,

R

Rome's empty stomach turned uneasily as he made his way out the door. By the time he arrived home, it was full-on nausea. He stopped in the driveway, his hands wet with sweat on the steering wheel. He sat there for what felt like forever.

"I can do this, I know I can do this," Rome said to himself. "This is no big deal." He'd already faced his own worst fears about himself. He'd had the courage to both fight and apologize to Ty. He'd even been brave enough to fall in love. This should be nothing after that! Though it certainly didn't feel like nothing.

Rome took slow, heavy steps to the door. His parents were waiting. They both must have taken the day off work. *That's not a good sign*, thought Rome.

He bit at his lip as they led him into the living room and motioned for him to sit. His mother's mouth was thin. His father's face was already getting flushed. "You want to explain yourself?" he started.

Rome was speechless. He wasn't sure what he was supposed to explain. His reaction to the fight? Swearing at them? Storming out? Staying out all night without letting his mother know where he was? After a while, his silence stood as well as any other answer could have done.

"Romeo, we know," said his mother. Rome's heart started beating faster than ever. He just stared down at his hands, trying to fight the heat building in his cheeks. What was that supposed to mean? What did they know?

His mother took out his phone and slid it across the coffee table. Rome's eyes went wide. His texts with Julian and Rosie, his late-night web searches, they must have seen all of it.

"Did those guys hit you on the head or something?" his father asked. Rome glanced up and was surprised to see a look of real concern on his father's face. Rome shook his head. Surely they must have seen that this had been going on since before his fight with Ty. "Come on, son," his father said, a touch of despair in his voice. "You're just so . . . so . . ."

"Butch, Dad?" Rome asked, crossing his arms.

"You're a man's man! I mean —" His father turned a deeper shade of red. "I mean, what about the team? And Marty? And Ben? Oh, you're not —" His father choked on his words.

A look of disgust crossed his mother's face. "You're not sleeping with them, are you?"

"Jesus," Rome groaned. His mother flinched at the word. *Sleeping with Ben and Marty? They can't really believe that!* thought Rome. He squirmed in his seat. This had to be the most uncomfortable conversation of all time. "Marty and Ben are my friends! Just friends!"

"Fine. So how do you think they're going to react?" asked his father, smugly.

"Not so well, I bet," his mother interjected.

Rome stared them down, silent, refusing to let them break him.

"We're just trying to protect you, Romeo," his mother said, more softly. "You have so much going for you." Turning back to Rome's father, she added, "You know, this wouldn't have happened if we went to church more often."

"Not now, Maria," his father shot back.

She fell silent. Rome felt bad. If only he could talk to his mother alone. He reached out, trying to comfort her, but she pulled away.

"Romeo, how can we trust you?" she asked. Her careful tone slipped, just for a moment. "Why did you lie to us?"

"When did I lie to you?!" Rome burst out. "I didn't know myself! It wasn't until Rosie started dating someone new, and then I met —"

"There it is!" His father smirked with satisfaction. "You and Rosie broke up! That's really what's going on, isn't it?"

"Romeo," his mother chimed in, "you know we

all love Rosie. But just because it didn't work out with her doesn't mean you can't meet another nice girl. You know, my old friend Margaret has a girl about your age. Maybe you could come to mass with me this week and meet her?"

"I've already met someone," Rome replied.

His mother let out a little huff.

His father scowled. "Whoever this sicko is, he's got you messed up in the head."

"How much do you even know about this . . . person?" asked his mother. "Is he older than you? Did he threaten you? Did he give you anything?"

"God, no!" Rome said. He could feel his chest tightening. "We're in love!"

"Oh, Romeo," his mother sighed. "Now I really know you've been brainwashed." She stepped into the kitchen and pulled out a bottle. As she poured herself a pre-noon drink, Rome's father called out to her and asked for one of his own. Rome endured a few minutes of insufferable silence, broken only by the sounds of glassware and pouring liquids.

"So is that where you've been?" his mother asked as she came back into the room, holding two drinks.

"What do you mean?" Rome gave her a sideways glance.

"Enough with the lies!" his father roared.

"We're not the fools you seem to think we are," his mother said. "You've been coming home late and avoiding my calls. So, we tracked your phone. We saw what neighbourhoods you've been in." She looked at him, her eyes wet with fear. "Are you doing drugs? Is that what this is about?"

"What?!" Rome's eyes went wide. He desperately wanted to tell them that Julian was sober. That he actually did all his drugs with his straight friends. But he decided better of it.

"We're scared for you, Romeo," his mother went on. "If this . . . If you're getting into trouble, you need to end it, now. You can't afford to lose everything you've worked so hard for."

Something inside Rome snapped. He couldn't hold himself back anymore. Rome felt his face flush red and his eyes began to sting. Looking back and forth between his parents, he stood. Wiping his tears on the sleeve of his jacket, he managed to say, "I know this is hard for you. But this doesn't have to be a big deal. There are even groups for parents and stuff." Rome pulled out the pamphlet from Lyla. Crumpled as it was, the rainbow flag on the cover still left little to the imagination. His father just glared at it, and then at Rome.

"You can't be serious." There was a hint of sarcasm in his mother's voice.

"That's it," Rome said, throwing the pamphlet on the floor. "I'm done."

As he moved to leave, his father snarled, "Sit back down."

Rome ignored him. This conversation was over. Just before he walked out the door, Rome glanced at his mother. "I'll come home, okay? In my own time."

With that, he was gone. This time, they didn't call after him.

Rome charged his phone in the car. He had a few missed calls and texts. They were mostly from Marty. He had gotten stitches in his lip, and had some sweet pain meds, which he was sharing with Ben over a couple early drinks. Sighing, Rome made his way over to join them. It wasn't even noon yet and it seemed he'd hit rock bottom. *Might as well keep digging*, he figured.

# 16 Cracking Open

"ROME'S HERE!" Marty called down to Ben as Rome swung the screen door open. The basement helped Rome relax a bit. It had that familiar shag carpet, musty smell, and old TV playing whatever happened to be on. Things felt a little more normal again.

Ben leaned back in one of the faded armchairs at a small round table covered in beer bottles and an over-flowing ashtray. He gave Rome a little wave. "Hey, man, if we can't go to school anyway, might as well party, right?" He flicked the lighter and started to pull on a joint. Rome shrugged.

"You okay, dude? Your eyes look puffy," said Marty. He spoke with a lisp from the stitches in his lip. "You got allergies or something?"

"Must be," Rome muttered. He thought of all the times he'd been here, just shooting the shit, playing a little cards. Mostly drinking and smoking and laughing over the good times.

The three settled into the old routine easily. With grad around the corner, there was still plenty to talk about. But the fight was all Marty and Ben wanted to discuss.

"That guy almost knocked your teeth out, Marty!" Ben remarked.

Marty grinned, showing off his braces. "Who woulda thought these would come in handy, right?"

The boys pushed each other around a bit, laughing. Rome felt more distant than ever, but his friends didn't seem to notice his mood.

"Made those ass-pirates run for it!" Marty

laughed. Turning to Ben, he raised an eyebrow. "Hey, remember you kissed a fag once? At Dyke Rosie's party? And don't say you were too drunk."

"Hey, shut up, asswipe, you want me to open up those stitches?" said Ben, laughing a bit too loudly. There was an ugly edge to it. Rome watched the two while pulling on a cigarette. "Hey, at least we never dated one, eh, Rome?" Ben said, redirecting the teasing.

"What?" Rome was shocked back into reality. He was suddenly sweaty and nervous. How did they know about Julian?!

"How is old Rug-Munch-Rosie, anyway?" Ben prodded. Marty chuckled beside him.

Rome let out a sigh of relief, then quickly changed the subject. "So you guys think they ended up calling the cops yesterday?"

"They better have!" Ben replied.

"Yeah, that guy almost knocked my teeth out!" Marty added.

Rome hesitated. He had to try to find the right

way to handle this. "But, like, you threw the first punch, right?"

His friends gave him odd looks, as if they were not sure what he was playing at. "I guess," Marty replied with a shrug.

Rome saw his chance. "Look, I'm just saying, let's just drop it, okay?"

"Oh, don't be so gay," said Ben, throwing his cigarette butt into the ashtray.

Rome felt himself go prickly. He wasn't in the mood to take any more shit. "Just lay off those guys, okay?" he said, staring Ben down.

Ben put up his hands, laughing. "Sounds like someone wants to lay on some guys. Am I right?" He and Marty high-fived and cheered their beers. Rome didn't change his stern expression. "All right, all right," Ben shrugged. "I don't want to talk to cops anyway."

Ben looked up at the ceiling. Rome felt a little more confident for having won at least this round.

Marty raised his eyebrows at Rome. "Something up?" he asked.

Rome looked down and fiddled with his class ring. The others were wearing theirs too. He'd always imagined the three of them growing older together. Going to the same school, maybe getting an apartment or going travelling. He thought they'd all settle down in the same neighbourhood, so their kids could be friends, too. *What else do I have to lose?* thought Rome. If any of those dreams had a chance of happening, his friends were going to have to learn to accept Julian as part of Rome's life. He answered them with a question. "Can I trust you?"

"You know it, bro," Ben answered, as if it shouldn't even be a question.

"What's the deal? You dying or something?" asked Marty.

"Guys . . ." Rome closed his eyes and took a deep breath. He didn't want to say it, but he couldn't stop now. "I'm . . . I met someone." They just looked at him, confused. "His name is Julian." The blank looks continued, so Rome made it perfectly clear. "I think I'm gay . . . or something."

"Yeah, right!" Ben said. He cracked up like it was the funniest joke he'd ever heard. Marty wasn't so quick to dismiss it. After a few seconds, Ben realized he was the only one laughing.

Squirming in the silence that followed, Rome looked down at his class ring again. As he twisted it around his finger, he knew the risk he was taking. If he lost them now, they'd probably never patch things up. But it was too late to back down. "He's really cool, honestly," Rome went on, trying to fill the space. "And when I'm with him I just feel —"

"Nasty!" Ben leaped up. "Oh, my God, why would you even tell me that?!" He started backing toward the stairs, making a face like someone let one rip. Rome tried to get up and follow him but, as soon as he got close, Ben pushed back. "Get off me!" Ben spat. "I can't believe you! We worked out together, we changed together. Were you jerking off to us all that time?!"

"It's not like that," Rome tried to say.

Ben wasn't sticking around to hear it. "Oh, shit, all those smokes we shared?! All the beers and shit! You probably gave me AIDS, you sicko!" Ben seemed more panicked than angry at this point. He was running away like a scared dog. "Stay away from me!"

The door upstairs opened with a creak and closed with a slam. Ben was gone.

Rome sighed. *Well, so much for keeping it a secret.* He doubted Ben would keep it to himself. There went Rome's whole high-school reputation. He saw that his one last friend was still seated at the table. Marty's face was blank, his joint was going out in a quiet flicker.

"I'll just . . . go," Rome said, moving to the stairs. At that, Marty stood up, as if jolted awake. Rome was unsure of what Marty was going to do. He prepared to defend himself as his friend came at him. It wasn't until he was a step away from Rome that Marty opened up his arms and wrapped Rome in a wordless, brotherly hug.

# 17 *Curiosity*

MARTY HAD A LOT OF QUESTIONS. Rome didn't have answers for everything. A lot of the questions made him feel equally confused.

"Like, how did you know, though?" Marty asked, still nursing his beer. "Like, you know?"

Rome shrugged. "I don't know."

"Come on." Marty waved his beer at Rome. "You gotta give me something."

"You really wanna know?" Rome asked, still unsure.

Marty just nodded. He relit the roach and offered Rome a pull. Rome shook his head, trying to focus on how to answer the question.

"I guess," Rome said, "the easy answer is, I knew when I met Julian. I mean, before that, I guess I kinda had thought about it. But I thought I was just being weird. I don't know. And then, bam."

"Just like that, eh?" Marty asked.

A goofy smile broke across Rome's face. "Yeah, just like that."

"What about you and Rosie?" Marty took a deep inhale and let it out in little puffs. "Did you know back then, too? Did she?"

Rome laughed. "Honestly? I think we both must have known, on some level. I mean, we were never really together like that anyway."

Marty's eyes widened, showing off his huge pupils. "You're kidding."

"Nah, man," Rome admitted. He sighed in relief. It really was all coming out now. "Everybody just thought we were!"

"Well, I guess that makes it a bit less surprising that she ended up being . . . you know . . ." Marty trailed off. He played with his lighter, flicking it on and off.

"Yeah," Rome answered. He watched Marty curiously. He hadn't seen his bud so out of it since the day after his bar mitzvah. He figured that Marty's high must be mixing funny with his beer.

"You know, I sometimes wonder," Marty mumbled, "if I'm, like, bisexual or some shit . . ." His words were even more jumbled because of his puffy lip.

"Oh?" Rome asked.

"Well, I don't wanna get with guys or anything but . . ." Marty looked around the empty room, as if the ashtray or grubby plastic plant in the corner might be listening. "I sometimes wear, you know . . . ladies' stuff." Marty studied his drink. "Do you do that?"

Rome stifled a laugh. This was a big secret to Marty, and it must have taken a lot of trust to share it, but it was shocking to imagine Marty like that. *I guess, at this point*, Rome figured, *nothing should really surprise me anymore.*

"No, I don't," Rome admitted. "But I think there's a lot straight guys who do that kind of thing."

"Don't you have gaydar or something?" Marty asked, looking desperate.

Rome shrugged. "I guess I could try?"

Marty looked up in excitement, only to go pale with fear. "Oh, wait, are you gonna try to kiss me?"

Rome reeled back. The thought of kissing Marty was disturbing, to say the least. And his messed-up lip didn't make it any more appealing. "No, idiot, I'm not gonna kiss you!"

Marty sat up, puffing up his shoulders. "Okay then. I'm ready."

"All right," Rome began. "Do you ever think about guys? You know, sexually? Would you wanna hook up with a guy? Like, make out, have sex, anything in between?"

Marty frowned. "No. I don't think so."

"Okay," said Rome. "Would you maybe wanna date a guy? Like, get romantic and all that?"

Marty shook his head again. "Probably not. I don't know . . ."

"What about girls?" Rome asked.

Marty blushed. "I mean, I'd be into it, if any of them were into me." He furrowed his eyebrows, looking like he was trying to solve a crossword while doing a handstand.

"Well, hmm," Rome said, puzzling things over. "Other than the dressing-up thing, what makes you think you might be gay, or bi, or whatever?"

Marty stared down his drink. "Well, at Rosie's party . . . there was this guy. At least I think he was a guy. He was hitting on me. I was kinda freaked out. And then Ben did his . . . whole thing. So we just took off." He looked up at Rome, even more desperate. "But I was thinking about it!"

Rome stood and offered Marty a hand. "Come on, let's get out of this house. I'm hungry, and it's stuffy in here."

Marty got up, a little unsteady, and they went out to the car.

"Dude," said Marty, the wind running through his hair sobering him up a bit. "Ben will get over it. You're still our Rome, he'll see."

Rome nodded, appreciative. Mostly because he thought it was nice that Marty seemed to really believe that.

Rome parked and they walked up to the pink awning outside Gayley's Café. This time, Rome smiled up at the name on the sign as they walked in.

They sat fiddling with the rainbow napkins and going over the menus. Marty looked around every few minutes, taking in the clientele. Rome chuckled a little. Was that what he looked like when he first came here? *God, he's so obvious*, Rome thought.

"What can I get you?" asked the waitress with a grin. She looked them both up and down. "First time here?"

Rome shrugged. It might as well be. He felt like a new man today.

"Wait, I know you from somewhere." Marty's eyes narrowed. "You're the boy from the party!"

Rome looked to Marty in confusion. Was he so gone he couldn't tell this was a waitress?

"Ha, wow! Small queer world! Yeah, hey!" the woman exclaimed. "You met me when I was in Guy-mode." She pointed to her name tag. "I'm Guyna, today."

Marty tripped over his words. "I'm, uh, I'm . . ."

"He's Marty," Rome explained.

Guyna laughed. She hit Marty on the shoulder with a friendly swat. "Right, Marty!"

"And I'm Rome," Rome offered.

"Cool, cool." Guyna grinned at him for a moment before turning her attention back to Marty. "Hey, look," she said, motioning to a unicorn-shaped clock on the wall, "I'm almost done my shift. How about I get you two some coffee and we'll chat?"

"Uh, can we maybe get some fries, too?" Rome

asked. "It might be good to soak up some of, uh, our liquid breakfast?"

Guyna wrinkled her nose in a laugh. When she came back to the table, she was carrying fries, pancakes, fruit, and large coffees.

In nearly no time at all, Guyna was recounting the most scandalous stories Rome had ever heard. "So he's trying to be all sexy, right?" she said. Marty and Rome nodded back in excitement. "And I'm just like, 'Um, buddy, that's my bellybutton!'" Marty and Rome roared with laughter.

Once the jokes and stories died down for a while, Marty broached a question. "So, uh, Guyna. You're a girl, right?" he asked. "But sometimes you dress up as a guy?"

"More or less." Guyna shrugged. "As much as I can, I try to just dress as myself. Sometimes I'm Guy. Sometimes I'm Guyna."

"Okay. But, like, why?" Marty prodded.

Rome went a little pink. He hoped that this kind of questioning wasn't out of line.

Guyna smirked. "I don't know, lots of reasons. Sometimes it's fun to mess with people. I get to play, like, little gendered tricks. It's funny to freak people out, or confuse them, or turn them on." She grinned at Marty with a knowing look. "Mostly, it's just for me. I just let myself be whoever I am that day!" She lowered her voice dramatically into a manly rumble. "You know what I mean?"

Rome glanced from Guyna to Marty and then back again, his head bouncing back and forth like he was watching a tennis match.

"Yeah, I do," Marty admitted. He grasped his glass of water and stared at the ice cubes inside. "And, um, do you like guys?"

"Most of them," Guyna replied. Her grin was mischievous. Reaching out, she put her hand on Marty's and raised her heavy eyebrows. "What about you?"

Marty audibly gulped and Rome held his breath. "Well, I . . ." Marty began, "I like girls. Well, most of them, and I . . ." Then he laughed. "I'm sorry, I've just honestly never even thought I'd talk about this before!" His laughter spread and all three giggled for a while. At last, Marty said, "I just never thought I'd meet anyone else even remotely like me."

"We're a special type," Guyna whispered.

As she leaned in closer to Marty, Rome started to feel like he was in the way. Thankfully, just then, his phone began to buzz. He leaped up when he saw the text was from Julian. Rome only stayed a second longer, just enough to see Guyna leaning over to whisper something in Marty's ear that made him turn a deep shade of red. Rome gave a little wave and slipped out the diner door. He was sure neither of them even noticed he was gone.

# 18 Stabbed in the Back

IT WASN'T UNTIL HE WAS BACK with Julian that Rome let himself feel the weight of all that had happened that day. He tried to joke about it at first. But his body began to shake as the reality of the fight with his parents and Ben's rejection came back at full speed. His knees buckled and he sat down on the steps to Julian's house. He stumbled over his words. "God, I'm so — I just —"

"Hey, hey, it's okay," Julian said in a soft,

comforting tone. "I'm here. You can cry if you need to."

Rome nodded, but tears didn't come. The two just hugged for a long while, until Julian suggested they go for a walk. Rome nodded again.

The night air rustled the shadows of leaves above with a gentle breeze. The couple wandered the streets, looking for somewhere quiet. When they passed an old graveyard, Julian suggested they head inside. Rome agreed, even though it gave him the creeps. Looking Julian over as he led the way in, Rome felt that familiar tingling electricity run through him. He blushed as Julian reached back for his hand. Laughing at himself, Rome knew, he would follow Julian anywhere.

"It's gonna work out," Julian said, squeezing Rome's hand. "With your folks I mean."

"Maybe," Rome replied. He studied the tombstones and watched the large stone angel that loomed over the little graveyard.

Julian shrugged. "Even if they don't come around, I'm here."

Rome blushed. Even if everything had fallen to pieces, a part of him was glad. He didn't want to have to be afraid of his feelings for Julian ever again.

Rome watched as the full moon's light cast dancing shadows across Julian's face. A warm feeling began to well up in his chest, moving into his cheeks and soon filling his whole body. As they talked, there was no longer any doubt. *This is real*, Rome told himself.

Julian looked at him with a smile. "I love you."

"I love you, too," said Rome. He kissed Julian's hand. "Honestly, all I want is to be with you." Without even thinking what he was doing, Rome slipped his class ring off his finger. He held it out to Julian as he got down on one knee. Rome knew this was too fast, too soon. But he didn't want to wait one more moment. "I know, not now . . . but one day," he asked, "Julian Capulet, would you marry me?"

Julian jumped in surprise. "Oh, Romeo!" he started. But any answer he might have given was cut short. A voice called out to them from behind. Rome stood and spun around. Three figures approaching from the street. One of them shouted in a menacing tone, "Hey, boys!"

Rome recognized them before they passed under a streetlight. Ben was in the lead, followed by Mike Veleno and Brad Morté. Those two were some of the biggest and baddest guys who had ever walked the halls of their high school. Rome didn't know them very well, but he'd played with them in summer baseball league. What were they doing here?

Ben gave a crooked smile.

*This isn't good*, thought Rome. "Ben, what are you doing here?" he called out.

"You're not so hard to find." Ben shrugged. Rome glanced down at Julian. A shiver of worry ran through his body and he took a step back. He had to get Julian out of there.

"Where you running off to, Ro-me-o?" called out Mike. The way he said Rome's name made his skin prickle unpleasantly.

Julian pulled at Rome's arm, but Rome didn't

move back any further. He refused to be intimidated. A hot wave of anger was building in his chest.

"I should have figured," said Brad. "You always did linger in the locker rooms, didn't you? Tryin' to look at my junk, eh, Rome? You wanna see my dick?"

Rome curled his nose in disgust.

As he came into full view, Brad slapped a baseball bat against his open palm. Rome eyed the weapon. A pang of sorrow mixed with the fury mounting inside him. The bat was the symbol of so many summer memories. Long days in the dugout, the taste of dust and sweat, laughter after a long game. Now all of that was gone, twisted into a threat.

"Ben told us how you tried to trick him," Brad spoke. "Trying to turn him sissy like you."

"Heard you messed up Rosie so bad, she thinks she's a dyke now!" Mike added. "What a damn waste."

Rome couldn't think of what to say, so he just looked at Ben. How could he just stand there, in his team jacket no less? Wasn't he supposed to be Rome's friend? Ben didn't even meet his eye.

He just looked down at his phone like this was a perfectly casual meeting.

"Come on, guys," Rome said, trying to reason with them. "You know it doesn't work that way."

As Mike and Brad got closer, Ben still stood, looking away.

"Come on! It's me!" Rome pleaded with Ben. "How can you —"

Rome didn't get a chance to finish his thought. Mike grabbed his collar and pulled back a fist, preparing to hit him square on.

Just then, Julian yanked on Rome, hard. He managed to slip Rome out of Mike's grasp. Julian and Rome began to run back toward the street.

"Only sissies run!" Brad called out.

"Pussy!" Mike echoed.

The words stung, but nothing mattered more to Rome than getting out of this with Julian alive. Rome was faster and got a few steps ahead. He reached back to grab Julian's hand, but he grasped at thin air. There was a cracking noise as the wooden bat smacked like it had just hit a home run. Rome spun and saw Julian falling while Brad prepared to strike a second blow. Ben just watched out of the corner of his eye.

Julian didn't move. But he didn't have to. Rome threw himself on the attackers. Acting completely on impulse and adrenaline, he knocked the bat out of Brad's hands. Rome got in a punch at Mike, aiming for his face but instead landing it in his beefy neck. Brad grabbed Rome by his shoulders and pulled him off Mike, throwing Rome against a broken gravestone. Rome felt a pang as his back hit it.

Fists were beating into him. Rome covered his face with his forearms. He looked in desperation at Ben, thinking *Please, don't do this*. But his so-called friend was already walking away.

As the punches turned to kicks, Rome coughed up something dark, warm, and wet. Every new pain only made Rome more furious. He wanted to punch back. He wanted to bite, to pull their hair out by its roots. He rolled onto his side and kicked out. He felt his foot land against Brad's crotch. That sent Brad falling back, shouting, clutching his groin. Mike paused for a second to see the damage done. Rome felt a moment of satisfaction. But it didn't last long. Both attackers turned back to Rome in an even greater rage.

Suddenly, from behind Mike and Brad, Julian appeared. He was holding the bat in both hands and swinging it wildly. He ran at Brad but, before he could land a hit, Mike stepped in. He socked Julian in the stomach, making him crumple with a whimper. Rome tried to get up but his body screamed in pain.

"Faggot," Mike spat at Julian. The word pierced the air. As Rome bled onto a stranger's grave, he wondered if that might very well be the last word he ever heard.

The two attackers turned back to Rome and began to kick again. Rome tried to see through their blows, tried to grab a glimpse of Julian. The world felt like it was turning upside down. He prayed silently, *Please, let Julian be safe.* Was it possible that Julian had escaped? A thought wormed its way into his mind. *Maybe he's already dead.* It was all so unreal. Could it just be some terrible dream? Had Julian ever even been there at all?

# 19 Recuperation

SOMEWHERE IN THE DISTANCE, Rome heard familiar voices. Someone was saying his name. "Where's Romeo?"

Rome winced as a smile rolled across his battered face. Julian was there, looking at him from a hospital bed next to Rome's own.

"You're alive," Julian gasped. His eyes welled up with tears.

"I promised . . . I wouldn't leave you," Rome croaked.

Angie was watching over them both. Moving to Rome's side, she pulled up his blankets and offered him some ice chips.

"How did we . . ." Rome tried to ask. But his throat was burning.

"Just rest," Angie said in her nurse's tone.

"We were worried when you didn't come back," came a voice from the other side of the room. Rome painfully rolled his head. There was his mother, sitting by the door. "We tracked your phone." She spoke in a tone that implied he should be thankful. Rome grimaced. Even if they had helped in the end, it still felt like a violation.

An awkward tension filled the room. Rome glanced from his mother, to Angie, to Julian. Finally, he rested his gaze on his own body. His torso was secured in some sort of plastic cast. His head felt heavy, like he hadn't had enough sleep. And his mouth was dry again already, despite the ice chips.

It was hard for Rome to stay awake. He was glad to find that no one expected him to. He drifted off, resting a little easier knowing Julian was next to him.

When Rome awoke again, Julian was still there and Angie was reading a book in one of the visitor's chairs. Rome's mother was gone. But soon enough, other visitors took her place.

Marty came in, looking sheepish. His head hung low as he cautiously approached Rome's bedside. "Hey, buddy," he said softly.

"Hey," Rome groaned back. "It's good to see you, man."

Marty's eyes were red. He was clearly on the verge of tears. Rome guessed it was probably not for the first time that day. "You too," Marty choked out before he started to break down. "I'm so sorry, Rome, I shoulda — I thought —"

Rome managed to give him a smile. "It's cool, Marty. It's cool."

"I always — I knew —" Marty tried to talk, his voice cracking every few breaths. "Ben could get, you know, but I never . . . I never thought . . ."

Rome nodded. "You know, it's not your fault."

Marty looked back up at Rome. A dribble of snot ran out his nose and came dangerously close to his busted-up lip. Jumping forward, he wrapped Rome in a big hug. Then he pulled back quickly when he realized how bandaged up Rome really was. "Oh, shit, I'm sorry, I —"

Rome winced and let out a laugh. "I'm glad you're here, dude." Even with Marty in such a somber mood, it was nice to have the company.

Marty managed to smile back, getting up to greet Julian. "I brought you guys a card," he explained, "From me and Guyna."

Rome smirked. *I guess those two spent a lot of time together last night, eh?*

The painkillers made Rome groggy again, and he happily slipped back into sleep. The times he woke up, Angie and Julian were always there. But his mother had yet to come back. He thought about asking Angie if she had been by while he was asleep, but decided against it.

Rome was pretty sure it was his second day in the hospital when Rose and Lyla arrived. They brought with them chocolates, pillows, and balloons. Rose instantly ran to Rome's side. She fussed over his cuts and bruises, saying, "Oh, Romie!"

"Hey, Rose," croaked Rome. "Thanks for coming."

"Of course!" she cried out. She put her hand over his arm. "Romie, you know I love you, right?" She gently patted his head. "You're like a brother to me!"

"Same," he managed to say, getting her to laugh.

Rose was full of stories and sweet treats, while Lyla chatted with Julian. "It's good to have company," Rome murmured before drifting back into his dreamless, painkiller sleep.

The next time he woke, he turned to watch Julian. Rome wished they could be closer. *I just wanna hold his hand*, he thought. His chest ached with desire — and probably also because of a broken rib or two. As he sank back into his pillow, there was a presence at his side. His mother was standing there. Her arms were crossed and she looked pensive.

"Uh, hi, Mom," said Rome.

She cautiously put her hand on his. Rome didn't want her close, but didn't want to push her away either. He felt Angie and Julian's eyes on them both.

"Romeo," she said, in nearly a whisper. "I knew this would happen."

"This. You knew this exact thing would happen?" Angie asked from across the room.

Rome smirked a little, thankful that Angie could say what he couldn't. His mother bristled, ignoring Angie and Julian.

*Why can't she just be a normal, comforting mother, for like five minutes?* Rome moaned internally. *Maybe she already did her five minutes, while I was passed out, and I missed it.*

"Mom . . ." His throat was dry as he tried to speak to her. "I'm . . ." He wanted to say he was sorry. But he caught himself, not sure what he was sorry for. Leaving after she and his father had refused to listen? Being in love with Julian? Being attacked by a couple of homophobic thugs led by his ex-best-friend? "Where's Dad?" he asked instead.

"He's not comfortable seeing you right now," his mother answered.

Rome felt his cheeks going red. *Not comfortable?* He didn't feel *comfortable*? Rome heard Angie huff in disapproval.

"Give him some time," said Rome's mother, gently squeezing his hand. He turned away, still furious, wanting nothing more than to pull away from her. But he couldn't bring himself to do it. And not just because he was all bandaged up. "I'm here," she told him. "And I love you."

Rome sighed and relented. "I love you too, Mom." Turning back, he swore he could see the hint of a tear in her eye.

"Rome!" A voice shouted from the door. Lawrence ran in and rushed to his bedside. He was followed by more footsteps, sharp sounds that were oddly familiar. "Do you need anything, buddy?" Lawrence asked, breathing heavily, like he'd run the whole way to the hospital. "Water? Food? More blankets?"

As Lawrence fussed over him, Rome saw his mother back away and hover awkwardly by the door. He wanted to call after her, but he was already getting sleepy again.

The guidance counsellor shook his head. "I always knew Ben had his troubles. And Mike and Brad certainly were a challenge when they were in school. But this . . ." Lawrence gave Rome a pained look. For a moment Rome felt tempted to comfort him. But then he was annoyed by the very impulse. He was quite done making other people feel better for this.

"I'm not surprised," Rome said simply. All fell silent for a while. Really, he wasn't.

"And . . ." Lawrence hesitated. "I'm sorry, but there's more bad news."

"What could be worse than this?" Rome asked.

Lawrence looked at Rome like he was an injured puppy. "It's your locker. It's been . . . defaced. We're fixing it as fast as we can, I promise."

Rome scowled. "What is their problem?" His body hurt, his head was pounding, his mouth was dry, and he was sick of this shit.

"This is just like when I went to high school," Julian sighed. "Maybe we're just not meant for it."

"Not if I have a say about it," said another voice. Suddenly, the stern face of the vice principal came into Rome's field of view.

Rome spoke up in surprise. "Mrs. Duke, what are you doing here?"

Julian turned to Rome. "You know her too?"

"She's the vice principal at my school. Wait — how do you know her?"

Angie snorted. "Don't you watch the news?"

Rome's head began to spin. This was too much to take in. Or maybe he was dreaming again. Mrs. Duke was saying something, apologizing for what happened. She seemed to be telling him something important. "Your suspension has been lifted," he heard, as if from a distance. "Clearly, we misunderstood the situation."

"Uh, thanks." Rome nodded.

"Mrs. Montague," said the vice principal. Rome blinked.He had nearly forgotten his mother was still standing there after all of Lawrence's fussing. Mrs. Duke turned, motioning to Julian's mom. "Angie." "Would you join me in the hall? I have something I'd like to discuss."

"If it's about us, just say it to us!" Julian piped up.

"I'm not so sure that's a good idea," Mrs. Duke was saying.

Rome couldn't hold on any longer. His body needed rest again. He welcomed the easy out from this bizarre situation.

## 20 Together

"ROMEO, are you awake?"

Rome's eyes blinked open. He smiled up at Julian. "I am now."

He could feel Julian's fingers running through his hair. Rome groaned a little in thanks. It was good to be close again.

"I talked to Mrs. Duke," Julian explained. "She had something she wanted to ask our moms. But I told them it should be up to us."

"What is it?" asked Rome. Right now, he'd do just about anything to stay close with Julian.

Julian leaned down and kissed Rome's head. "Oh, my Romeo," he whispered. "I'm so glad . . . I was so scared you were . . ."

Rome breathed in Julian's sweet smell and let it out in a little sigh. "Me too." He watched Julian's eyes, basking in their deep, warm brown. Everything would be all right, as long as they could be together. He almost didn't want to break the moment, but Julian had piqued his curiosity. "What did they want you to ask me?"

"Right," said Julian. "Well, you know how my mom does all that political stuff?"

"Yeah." Rome nodded.

"She and Joanna Duke — I guess Mrs. Duke to you — they've been doing this big thing," Julian explained. "A campaign, trying to get schools in Duke's division to have a course on gender and sexuality and stuff, something to make it easier for . . . people like us."

Rome managed to shrug a little. "Cool."

"Yeah." The hint of a smirk crossed Julian's face. "Kinda cool. And they want us to help. They've got some big rally on Saturday, and they want us to be there. Maybe to take pictures and say something to the crowd."

Rome's stomach turned. "And, uh, what do you think?"

"Well, I don't know. My mom was pretty into it. No surprise. Your mom, not so much."

"No surprise." Rome tried to smile through his nerves. "Well, do you want to?"

"It's kind of scary, don't you think? Putting ourselves out there like that. I've never done anything like it before." Julian started playing with Rome's hair again.

Rome reached for Julian's hand. "I know you could do it," he said as they intertwined their fingers.

Julian smiled and glanced down at Rome's bandaged body. "I don't want to make you do anything you're not ready for. And, I mean, what if somebody you know saw us?"

"I don't care." Rome's voice was firm.

Julian looked up at him, eyes wide. "Really? But what about . . . ?"

Rome pulled Julian's hand to his chest and rested it over his heart. "I'm not afraid anymore. I mean, I'd say things have gone pretty much as bad as they could." They both chuckled a little. "But the good news is, I really don't care anymore. I just want us to be together. And I want to be brave, like you."

Julian kissed his cheek. "Are you sure?"

Rome nodded. It didn't matter if people didn't understand. He didn't even care if his parents didn't come around. He was going to be okay. "You make me better at being me," said Rome, holding Julian close. "I want to do it. Let's show everyone how strong love can really be."

Julian nodded and gave Rome a shy smile. "Okay, let's do it. Let's go out there and change the world."

"Together," Rome agreed.

# Acknowledgements

So many people made this book possible — including you, the reader! Thanks so much for helping this story come to life!

I'd like to give special appreciation to Shane Camastro, for supporting the stories of Romeo & Julian, even when they were still just daydreams.

A big hug for Kat Mototsune — thank you for editing this text. Your support, guidance, and kindness were all essential for my writing process.

Thank you to Louis Esmé. Your feedback on this story was essential. I will forever be thankful for both your honesty and friendship.

Bridget Liang, your collaboration and comradeship made writing so much richer! I know you will continue to make amazing things.

Much love to all the Phoenix Nest — past, present, and future! Thank you for taking care of each other, laughing together, and living out all that real love can be.

Thanks to all my holos back in the day in Winnipeg. You were the best friends a messed up teen like me could ever ask for. And special shout out to Ariyanna - you'll always be my big sister.

Thank you, Iris Robin, for all your comments, questions, ideas, and enthusiasm! You're a truly fabulous friend.

Many thanks to Kate Welsh, your brainstorming sessions and helpful ideas are all over this work.

Sienna Rachelle — many thanks to you, and all your family, for being absolutely weird and wonderful.

All my love to Andrew McAllister — your companionship means the world to me. And to Hannah Dees — I can't wait for us to start our family together.

Finally, Bill & Cheryl Telford, Tony Harwood-Jones, and Heather Dixon. You have both literally and figuratively made me who I am today. Thank you for everything.

MN
&
YA1